The Moon King

'Written sensitively and beautifully, *The Moon King* is
sure to be another winner'
DUBLIN ECHO

'Siobhán Parkinson is a cunning and practiced hand at
storytelling, and getting under her characters' skin, and
this is a dead cert for readers from ten upwards'
BOOKS IRELAND

'Original and fascinating story ... stylishly and
thematically, Parkinson's novel credibly demonstrates
the power of the imagination to reshape and transform
experience'
THE IRISH TIMES

'A sensitive portrayal of a child's struggle to
rebuild his life'
BEST BOOKS

Special Merit Award to The O'Brien Press
from **Reading Association of Ireland**
*'for exceptional care, skill and professionalism in
publishing, resulting in a consistently high standard in all
of the children's books published by The O'Brien Press'*

SIOBHÁN PARKINSON

Siobhán lives in Dublin with her woodturner husband
Roger Bennett and her schoolgoing son Matthew. She
has worked in publishing as an editor is now
writer-in-residence at the Irish Writers' Centre.

OTHER BOOKS
by Siobhán Parkinson

Sisters ... No Way!
Overall winner Bisto Book of the Year

Four Kids, Three Cats, Two Cows, One Witch (maybe)
Winner of a Bisto Book of the Year Merit Award

Amelia
No Peace for Amelia

For older readers
Breaking the Wishbone

And for younger readers:
The Leprechaun Who Wished He Wasn't
All Shining in the Spring

THE
Moon King

Siobhán Parkinson

THE O'BRIEN PRESS
DUBLIN

First published 1998 by The O'Brien Press Ltd.
20 Victoria Road, Rathgar, Dublin 6, Ireland.
Tel. +353 1 4923333 Fax. +353 1 4922777
e-mail: books@obrien.ie
website: www.obrien.ie
Reprinted 1999 (twice)

ISBN 0-86278-573-1

British Library Cataloguing-in-publication Data
Parkinson, Siobhán
The moon king
1. Foster children - Juvenile fiction
1. Children's stories
I. Title
823.9'14 [J]

3 4 5 6 7 8 9 10
99 00 01 02 03 04 05 06

The O'Brien Press receives
assistance from

The Arts Council
An Chomhairle Ealaíon

Typesetting, layout, editing, design: The O'Brien Press Ltd.
Cover separations: C&A Print Services Ltd.
Printing: Caledonian International

For Matthew and Benjamin
and Matthew and Benjamin

AUTHOR'S NOTE

The moon chair shown on the cover is based on chairs made by the furniture-maker Paul Berg. The idea for this book came from a chance remark made by Cyril Forbes, former chairman of the Crafts Council of Ireland, talking about a Paul Berg chair.

The characters and events in this book are entirely fictitious, but the tall house with the sloping garden and the attic really exists. The real house is in Cork, but the house in the story is in an imaginary town.

CONTENTS

CHAPTER 1

Spiderboy and the Lipstick Woman

Up and up. Pain in your throat and back of your neck from looking up. Can't see tiptop of roof from here. Tall gate, and thin. Iron. Bars. Like cage. All those steps. So high. Steps climb up through garden. Grass all tilted down, like carpet out to dry. Good for rolling. Terrible for football.

The woman creaked the gate open and beckoned to Ricky to come with her. Reluctantly, Ricky stepped through the open gate, onto a little concrete platform, where the garden steps began. The woman pushed the gate closed behind them. She gave Ricky a gentle push, and he started up the steps, toiling up and up through the steep, down-tilting garden. He stopped on a little concrete landing, halfway up. Whew! Then came more steps, and more climbing.

At the top, near the front door, the final step opened out onto a smooth area with a park bench and a chimney-pot full of pink flowers – the ones with the musty smell, geraniums – in front of the house. Ricky had never seen such a big high house before, with such tall windows.

He could have stood on the windowsill and his head would still have been lower than the middle bar, where the upper and lower pane met. Not that he would do such a thing. It was probably the people's living-room window. Or maybe not. It was more like a store-room. Anyway it was full of things, absolutely choc-a-bloc with things – furniture, things that looked like hatstands, things that looked like very large and heavy electrical appliances from the fifties, toys, car-tyres, even a bicycle.

The woman was ringing the doorbell. Ding-dong, said the house, out of its deep belly. Ding-dong. There were noises inside, rustlings, people unwrapping themselves, thumps, shrieks, laughter, shouts. Ricky felt nervous.

Want hide. Look at wall. Wall friendly. White, with cracks. Spider scuts out one crack, into another crack. All legs, spiders. Shoulders hunched. Busy, busy, busy.

Suddenly Ricky crouched down, knees bent, ears hidden, elbows out, facing the wall of the house.

'Ricky! Stand up, now, there's a good boy.' The woman's voice came from way above him.

Won't stand up. Not good boy. Spider. Spiderman. No. Spiderboy.

Flap-flap said the door of the house, opening into the dark. Ricky could just see all the dark inside the house from where he hunkered by the front wall. He looked away. He didn't want to see in. He was Spiderboy. He

10

wished he had a crack to scuttle into, like the real spider. Then whoof! the woman bent down beside him. There was a smell of lipstick and the sound of beads clicking right in his ear. He clamped his hands tightly over his ears, but he could still hear her voice, the voice of the lipstick-smelling woman, like a voice under water: 'Come on, now, Ricky. It's OK. Really it is. This is a nice family.'

Don't like nice families. Don't like families. Don't like big tall houses. Don't like grass rolls down garden. Terrible for football. Don't like living room all hatstands. Bicycle OK though. Like bikes.

'Please, Ricky,' said the woman gently.

Ricky unbent and stood up slowly, unclamping his ears. Fearfully, he looked towards the front door. A large, comfortable woman, like a well-stuffed sofa in a dress, stood in the doorway. Her fair hair grew at all angles out of her head and went wandering off in every direction, but her eyes were looking straight at Ricky and smiling at him. As soon as he caught her eye, he looked quickly away, and let his gaze wander around and behind her into the house. Like the room he had seen through the front window, the hall was full of stuff. Even the stairs were piled high with things on both sides, with only a narrow channel of space for going up and down. There were cardigans, books, socks, envelopes, a hairbrush with clumps of blond, brown and red hair clinging to it, unidentifiable wooden objects, dog-eared photographs, a biscuit tin full of dusty sea-shells, roller skates. And the stairs themselves went up and up into the dark. Ricky could just make out a rocking chair at the top of the stairs, but he couldn't see any further; after that, it was just dark.

The large woman at the door didn't say anything for a moment, but she continued to beam at Ricky. Then a door flew open somewhere behind her and it was as if somebody had let the lid off a pressure cooker. A riot of children came tearing down the hall, shrieking and yelling, pulling at one another's clothes, tripping each other up. It looked like some sort of crazy race with no rules. One tall girl kept shouting, 'Go easy, go easy, mind the small ones!' but she was sobbing with giggles as she said it and it didn't seem to make much impact.

Hearing the rumpus, the large woman turned to face the avalanche of children. 'Whoa!' she ordered, and the children slithered and slipped more or less to a halt, but they continued to writhe and punch each other and the noise level didn't go down much. Expertly, the woman, the mother she must be, plucked the smallest children out of the mêlée and pulled them to safety around her skirts. The very tiniest – a little scrap of a boy that danced and jigged in bright green dungarees, with pale hair all fluffed out from his head like a dandelion clock – she scooped into her arms and kissed several times.

By now the babble of children's voices and the scufflings and thumpings had subsided enough for the mother's voice to be heard.

'Come on, everyone. Back to the kitchen. We've got visitors to entertain.'

The seething mass of children started to bubble and splutter with excitement as they scrabbled to their feet and turned back the way they had come, the voices of the biggest calling: 'Biscuits! We've got visitors, so it'll be biscuits.'

The hub-bub died away as the main body of children disappeared into the back of the house, but the littler ones kept up a small, persistent clamour, which rose in pitch at the mention of biscuits. 'Bikkies, bikkies, bikkies,' they squawked, as if they only ever got biscuits at Christmas, dancing away ahead of their mother into the dark of the hall.

Ricky and the woman with the lipstick followed the large woman down the dark hall and into a big bright green-and-white kitchen, where the sun came pouring in in such a stream that you felt you could wash your hands in it. There were pools of sun everywhere, and sun squares on the table, warm yellow squares of sunshine.

The mother started making coffee, the warm sweet smell filling the sunny room. The children had suddenly gone quiet, as if they had worn themselves out with their earlier rowdiness. Even the small ones had stopped dancing and had settled quietly on chairs and stools and on the floor, like butterflies with their wings folded. Now that they had stopped knocking each other about and shouting at each other, they seemed finally to notice

Ricky. They were watching him.

'Sit down, son,' said the mother, pouring water onto the coffee grounds. 'Not there. Helen, move those newspapers, like a good girl.'

With a loud sigh, the girl called Helen picked up an armful of newspapers from a chair and dumped them with a thump on the floor. Nobody seemed to mind.

'Here,' said the mother, then, swishing her hand across the seat of the chair, as if to dust it off, 'sit here, Ricky. Now, who'd like a biscuit? One each now, *one*, do you all hear that?'

'*One*,' the smaller children told each other solemnly, raising their index fingers to one another.

A plate of funny flat biscuits, with shapes on them, like writing, appeared. Ricky bit into his. It tasted warm and sweet, almost like the smell of the coffee. The mother and Lipstick Woman were talking now. 'Aphasia,' Lipstick Woman hissed. 'Dyslexia?' asked the mother. 'Dysfunctional,' whispered Lipstick Woman. 'Place of safety.' 'Of course,' said the mother with a nod. Ricky looked from one to the other, wondering vaguely what the words meant.

The smallest child, the one with the dandelion-clock hair, offered Ricky another biscuit. He shook his head.

Don't want no more biscuits. Want go on bike. Want go home. Can't go home. They won't let you. Don't want go home anyway, not really, not now. Home bad place now.

14

'This is your home, now, Ricky,' Lipstick Woman was saying. 'For the moment. Until ... until things change.'

Don't like change. Want go home. No. Don't want. What then?

There was that lipstick smell again and the sound of beads clicking as Lipstick Woman bent close to Ricky. 'I'll be back to see you in a few days,' she said. 'Won't that be nice?'

No. No. Won't be nice. This house too full things. Too full people you don't know. Too tall. You won't be able to find your way to top. And if you do, you'll fall. How can it stay standing, up on hill like this? Why doesn't topple over? It will. It will. It will topple over. As soon Lipstick Woman leaves, it will topple over, crumple up, and all these children and mother and hatstands and hairbrush and Spiderboy will all be squashed to bits, like big heap rubble. Oh no! No! Can't stay here this big house all strange people. No!

Flap-flap said the door as the two women left the kitchen. As soon as the door closed, the children dived on the plate of biscuits, all jostling for illicit extra goodies. Then, stuffing biscuits into their mouths and into their pockets and up their sleeves and giggling at their own daring, they lurched to the door and followed the two women into the hall. They skipped down the hall and into the front living room, the one Ricky had seen through the window from the garden, to spy on Lipstick Woman leaving. Ricky trailed after them, watching as they found places to perch between the hatstands and things, all clamouring to get a view. They clustered around the window, like roses around a doorway, watching Lipstick Woman climbing down the garden, nodding and laughing, jostling and elbowing each other and munching their sweet spicy biscuits. Ricky stood miserably behind them.

Want mother.

Then the mother came in and whooshed the children away from the window. 'Come,' she said to Ricky, holding out her hand. 'Come and help me to get your bed ready.'

CHAPTER 2

Dandelion Girl Meets the Banshee (or Not)

Something woke Rosheen that night. She was a light sleeper. She was used to all the creakings and rustlings of the old house turning over in its sleep by now, so these things didn't wake her any more, but strange sounds woke her, and this was a very strange sound. She sat up sleepily, her fair hair tangled like a web before her eyes, her eyelashes prising reluctantly apart, and listened. There it was again. A sort of high-pitched yowl, a bit like a cat's night lamentings, but not exactly that either.

Could be a banshee, thought Rosheen, swinging her pink feet out from under the duvet, and feeling for her slippers. Lucky she slept on the bottom bunk. Helen had fought for the top and won, but now Rosheen was glad. Being on the bottom gave her more freedom. A banshee would be good. The others would be dead impressed. She pushed the web of hair back off her forehead with a sleep-dampened hand and rubbed her eyes good and hard, to make sure she was fully awake. If she was going in search of a banshee, she'd better be awake and able to see properly. She patted the bed, searching in the dark for her bright yellow dressing-gown, and struggled into it.

Rosheen crept along the wall to the door, and eased it open. The dim yellow glow of the landing nightlight filtered into the room, but Helen didn't stir. Lazy lump. You couldn't wake her if you tried. Rosheen stifled a giggle. Funny how being awake when someone else was asleep made you feel stronger than they were. Rosheen wouldn't dare even to think like that when Helen was awake. Helen was supposed to be her friend – they were almost the same age – but sometimes she was hard to like, and today had been one of those times.

Rosheen closed the door carefully behind her, the triangle of light on the bedroom carpet gradually diminishing till it was just a crack, and then at last the door fitted into place and the seal against the light was complete.

She pressed her back against the door, arching her neck so that as much of the back of her head as possible touched the door, and, jamming her calves into a straight line against the wood, she listened again for the sound. This was how people creeping about furtively at night were supposed to behave. She knew from watching films on the telly. She wondered whether she looked sufficiently dramatic in her lemon dressing-gown with her hair mussed up and one hand behind the small of her back, the fingers spread out against the door. She cocked her head, and sure enough, as if on cue, there came the yowling sound again. It was coming from downstairs, she thought.

Rosheen bent over and ran with her bottom in the air and using her hands as forepaws, as if dodging bullets. This was cool fun. When she got to the stairs, she grasped the banister rail for dear life and edged down from step to step, keeping her feet carefully on the varnished edge of the stairs, between where the strip of stair carpet ended and the banisters began. If she stepped on the carpet, the banshee would catch her. When she arrived at the last step before the hall, Rosheen wavered. She would have to step on the dreaded carpet now, banshee or no banshee, because here the floor was completely carpeted, with no wooden margin. She closed her eyes and leapt into the air. It was like diving off a whaling ship. It was like launching into space. It was like swimming into the stratosphere. Goodness knows where she would end up.

She landed with a thump, feet first, outside the living-room door.

Then came the high-pitched yowl again, much closer now. There could be no doubt about it. It was coming from inside the living-room door. What did banshees look like? Rosheen wondered. They combed their hair, she thought, or was that mermaids?

Gingerly, she pushed the door open, half-expecting to see a ghostly woman combing her ghostly locks in the moonlight, but of course there was no such thing, just a lot of dark shapes and an irregular ridge under the covers of a makeshift bed that Mammy Kelly had somehow constructed for the new boy, because he wouldn't climb the stairs. He'd stood in the hall, gazing up at the half-landing, and resolutely resisting encouragement to go up. He was a funny lad. Didn't say a word. In the end, Mammy Kelly said he could sleep downstairs, just for tonight, until he got used to the house.

Rosheen was secretly relieved there was no banshee, but she wouldn't admit it for the world and was busy making one up to tell the others about in the morning when the eerie yowling came again. It filled the room. It sounded much weirder close up like this, like an animal in pain, lifting its maw to the skies and bewailing its plight to the moon. Rosheen yelped without meaning to, and the smudge on the pillow shot up in the air. The ridge under the covers flattened and there was Ricky, sitting bolt upright, his hair standing about his head like a chimney brush and his face white in the yellowy light from the hall.

Ricky stared. He'd been dreaming about the small child with the dandelion-clock hair. He'd dreamt that somebody had puffed at the child's head the way you blow a dandelion-clock and that the child's hair had drifted apart, like a dandelion clock. There were dandelion seeds everywhere floating and drifting, like aerodynamic cottonwool, in his dream. But this wasn't a dandelion seed. This thing that had appeared in his room was yellow, all shimmery, maybe a fully grown dandelion, and it shook with bubbly laughter, its yellow hair all bobbing and its shimmering yellow gown falling in butter-yellow folds onto his bed.

'You were snoring!' snorted Rosheen. 'I thought you were a banshee!' And she was off into ripples of laughter again.

Ricky smiled uncertainly. He didn't know what a banshee was, but that didn't surprise him. Words often evaded him. He nodded at the dandelion, bobbing and wafting at the foot of his bed. Then he lay back carefully on the pillows and stared at his surroundings, all the wooden things looming in the dark at him, the handlebars of the bicycle gleaming in the light that flooded in from the open door.

'I'm sorry. You're tired. I'll go.'

The dandelion girl stood up. Ricky nodded again. She bent over him. 'I'm Rosheen,' she whispered. 'Good night.'

And she was gone, the door following her into the dark. Good night. Good night.

CHAPTER 3

Breakfast in the Tall House

Breakfast was a rowdy affair in the tall house. Mammy Kelly stood in the hall and smote a mighty brass gong that looked as if it must have come from some Indian temple, and she was answered by shufflings and scuttlings and yelps from several storeys up, and presently an assortment of children, some of them Kellys, some not, came trooping down the stairs in mismatched pyjamas and outgrown nighties and tracksuit-trousers that would have to do, worn, as often as not, with somebody else's T-shirt.

Mammy Kelly was a believer in a good breakfast. There was a steaming pot of porridge, mounds of fluffy scrambled eggs and soggy halves of grilled tomatoes and a battered silver toast-rack laden with triangles of pale brown toast. There was a large pot of weak tea at each end of the table (strong tea not being healthy for young bones, according to Mammy Kelly) and a small pot of rich-smelling coffee, for Mammy Kelly herself, whose health was beyond rescuing, as she said comfortably to anyone who cared to enquire.

Ricky, asleep in his campbed in the living room on

that first morning, heard the gong in his dream. It had a soft, dull, resonating voice, such as an elderly musical bear might have, and he turned over at the sound, wondering fuzzily what it meant. Then he heard the tripping of feet down the stairs, and this sound wasn't in his dream any more. He edged up on the pillow and listened. Feet continued to flap and patter past his door, dozens of feet it seemed. He opened his eyes. Strange wooden things, hatstands, stared at him, hulking in the half-light that escaped through the curtains. The tall, tall house. Of course. That's where he was. At the very bottom of it, and now all the creatures were coming down the stairs, creeping and tumbling and skipping down, and the top of the house hadn't fallen over in the night, as it hadn't fallen over any other night in the past hundred years since it had been built.

He tried to think about the feet and who they belonged to. What sort of creatures. Dandelions, he thought. Roses. He shook himself. Children. It was children. That was the word. And then he knew. As soon as he found the word, he knew that he was going to have to get up and be one of those children.

At that thought, he tunnelled under his blankets and stopped his ears with his pillows. The dark down there was warm and comforting, and Froggo was with him there. He could hear muffled laughs from the next room, though. They were sure to be laughing at him.

The door opened with a creak. Oh no! They weren't

going to make him come now, were they? Ricky sat up. The pale grey light of the hall invaded the dark room. Something shimmered in the greyness. Rosheen. The name popped into his mind from nowhere and startled him with its sureness. How could he possibly know this shimmer-creature's name? He had never seen her in his life before.

He lay down again quickly so he wouldn't have to look at her. Spiderboy. He was Spiderboy, and he had things to do, webs to spin, cracks to scuttle into.

'Mammy Kelly says your breakfast is ready,' said Rosheen to the bump on the bed that was Ricky.

She waited for a moment or two, but the new boy didn't say anything.

'Come on then, so. Where are your slippers? Or have you slippers? People usually have when they arrive, but they don't last. Lauren had hers for two weeks. Billy's disappeared on his very first day. I don't remember if I had any. I've been here since I was ... oh, I don't remember, very small anyway.'

Ricky sat up again and looked at Rosheen.

'No slippers?' said Rosheen.

Spiderboy nodded.

'Is that a yes or a no?'

Spiderboy nodded again.

'I mean, is it yes you have no slippers, or is it no you have no slippers?'

Spiderboy nodded again.

'Or yes you have slippers?'

Spiderboy stared.

'Oh come cn anyway. The toast will be getting soggy.'

Spiderboy looked under his bed, to make sure he had no slippers. He checked under the covers. No slippers. Only Froggo. He shoved Froggo further down under the blankets, in case Rosheen saw him, and eased himself out of bed.

'Dressing-gown?' asked Rosheen.

Spiderboy stared.

'Here, use this,' Rosheen said, and threw his anorak at him.

Spiderboy nodded.

And Rosheen danced out into the morning light of the hall and into the sounds of breakfast, with Ricky, awkward in his anorak and too-short pyjamas, trailing behind her.

CHAPTER 4

Up into the Dark

Ricky survived breakfast by sitting still and eating only the food that was put directly in front of him. He didn't dare to stretch out for anything beyond his immediate grasp. Not that there was any need to be nervous. The other children had no intention of fighting him for toast or the marmalade jar. It was just that he was nervous because he wasn't used to so many people and loud noises made him jump. He couldn't get it out of his head that when somebody shouted it meant he was in trouble. At home, he had nearly always been in trouble anyway, whether people were shouting at him or not. He certainly wasn't used to people just shouting so they could be heard over the din all the other people were making.

He was glad when they all clattered off to school, in a babble of screeches and last-minute panics about missing homework copies and hockey socks. All except the mother and the smallest child, the one with the dandelion-clock hair – the little boy in dungarees who was called Billy. And Ricky of course. Nobody suggested he should go to school. The front door closed with a boom after the last of the children, and Ricky could hear their voices still raking the air as they scuffled and rolled and shrieked their way down through the steep garden. Gradually the sounds faded away, and peace descended on the tall house.

Mammy Kelly was sloshing away at the sink, washing up and humming to herself. Billy sat on the floor amid the debris of breakfast with his little legs stretched straight out in front of him and quietly ate a sticky crust that had fallen off the table, examining his plump fingers between bites with great interest. Ricky wandered into the hall and looked up the stairs, into the dark at the top of the house. There were things all the way up the stairs, and at the top, on the half-landing, there were more things, books mainly.

Books, everywhere books. Do they read them? Who does? Why do they?

High up in the dark, among the books, Ricky could make out the outline of a rocking-chair.

Your mother had rocking-chair. Warm and swaying, in your mother's arms, like big, warm, branchy tree. Rock, rock, rock. Like fast train, so fast you can't feel ground speeding by, but carriages rock, rock, nice, like sleeping. Must have been very small then. Before all that anyway, before Ed and everything. Wish, wish.

Ricky longed to climb up to the rocking-chair, but he was afraid of the stairs and afraid of the dark. The dark was like a big, damp blanket, and there were sure to be things

27

in the shadows, looking at him, watching, waiting to pounce on him.

Thump! There! That'll larn ya! Leave off, Nancy. He hasta learn manners. No-o-o! No-o-o! Oh please, no. You didn't do it. You didn't mean it. Stop! Please, please, no-o-o!

In a panic, his heart throwing itself against his ribs, Ricky searched for the light switch to make the things in the shadows go away. This one? No. This one? Yes, this one. The light came on and suddenly Ricky could see all the way up the stairs to the rocking-chair. He could see that there was nothing at all waiting or watching or getting ready to pounce. It wasn't scary any more, now the light was on. Maybe he could try it.

Come on, Froggo. Twelve stairs, maybe fourteen. You can manage. Up, up, up.

Ricky climbed cautiously up the stairs, stepping carefully between all the toys, books and clothes that lined the staircase, taking care not to disturb any of them. At last he reached the rocking-chair at the top of the first staircase. Gingerly, he sat into the deep cushioned seat.

Whoo! Hold on, Froggo. Close your eyes. Back and forth, back and forth, like rowing boat, like garden swing, swaying in air, no feet, like swimming, no weight, like being in cloud, like *being* cloud, bird, like flying, skimming, like spinning on web-thread, Spiderboy spinning, spinning, whooshing, whoom! Bang! What? Where? Oh! Dark again.

Panic leapt in Ricky again, till he realised that it was just that somebody had switched off the light. He heard steps in the hall, and humming. Mammy Kelly had found the light on and just switched it off automatically. She wasn't to know that Ricky was crouched up there in the dark, terrified.

Dark is everywhere. Watch out! Door behind you.

But it was only the bathroom door, Ricky knew, because he could smell the crisp sweet smell of toilet cleaner. There was nobody in the bathroom. He knew that really.

But somebody could. They could, yes.

Ricky blinked, trying to force the panicky feelings down into his stomach. He made himself sit still and look carefully around him. He knew that if he concentrated the dark wouldn't seem so black. He blinked again. There! it wasn't really too dark, it was only a daytime dark, just grey. Those shapes were books, on bookshelves, nothing worse than that. There were books everywhere in this house. It was like some sort of mad library on a hill.

Rock, rock, very gently. You can close your eyes now, and swoop like a crow.

When he opened his eyes again, and looked around a

little, he could see that there were more stairs, going up again, into more dark, and that there were more things on those steps too. Craning his neck a little, he could see up to the next landing, and he could make out doors up there. Is that where Rosheen sleeps, up there? he wondered. That door? Or that one?

Suddenly a door creaked open up there and the panic started again. Ricky wanted to leap out of the rocking chair and flee down the stairs but he was afraid of breaking something on his way down. So instead he sat very still, wishing the door would close again, that whoever had opened it would change their mind.

Oh Froggo! Sit very still. Head between knees. Close your eyes. Still, still, don't breathe. Hope. Just hope. Whoosh, whoosh, steps coming down, down, nearer. Whump. Large body. Thumps down behind you.

Ricky kept his eyes tightly shut, still willing the person to go away, but then came a voice in his ear, a big, boomy voice saying 'Good morning.' The voice was so big it seemed to echo in Ricky's chest.

A man.

Holding his breath with fear and with his eyes still tightly closed, Ricky slid off the chair, and then slithered on his back down the stairs, bump, bump, stair by stair, bump, bump. But he'd forgotten about all the things lining the staircase, and within seconds he had started an avalanche of cardigans, coat-hangers, a doll with hard

30

arms, books. Everything was loosening, more books were dislodged, their pages fanning out and getting crushed and crumpled. Ricky arrived in a heap in the hall, a tangle of limbs and things. His bottom hurt and he'd banged his funny bone, but as soon as he reached the hall he jumped to his feet, looking quickly for the door of the room where he'd slept the night before. Quickly, quickly, quickly, his heart said. He threw himself at the door, slammed it shut once he'd got inside and slithered to the floor. Safe.

Knock, knock.

Spiderboy not home.

Ricky slithered under the bed.
Knock, knock, 'Hello?'

Lie flat, don't breathe.

Cre-eeak, said the door. Clump, clump, clump. A big person came into the room.

'Ricky?' This man had such a big, booming voice, like Santa Claus.

Spiderboy fine here under this bed.

Creeeeee-eeeak, said the bed, moaning.

The Santa Claus person sat on the bed. Ricky could see his boots, big, big boots. Then he shut his eyes again and waited for the big man to go away.

Don't look, eyes tight. Spiderboy in this crack here.

'Only, I was hoping you might be able to help me.'

Help? Help? Spiderboy can't help. Spiderboy sleeping now.

'There's this amazing heap of things in the hall. They didn't look so much when they were spread out on the stairs, but when they all came tumbling down and landed in one big pile in the hall – you wouldn't believe the amount of stuff there is.'

Heaps? Stuff?

'There's cardigans and books and photographs and a doll with no head and somebody's runners and a basket of dried flowers (spilt) and a few more books and a hairbrush and three packets of toothpaste (unopened) and what looks like my favourite mug that's been missing for the past three weeks and could do with a wash, and I think I can see five socks, none of them with mates, and any number of bills, still in their envelopes, about forty-five assorted pens and pencils, bits of paper, drawings, seashells, computer disks (which is funny, because we haven't got a computer), a bottle of wine (unopened, and more to the point, unbroken), half a Toblerone (that's even better than the wine), one wellington boot, too small to fit anyone in this house except Billy and it's too big for him, a bicycle bell, two lipsticks, a few more books, and a whole laundry basket full of clothes – clean, but not ironed (well, one out of two ain't bad).'

Ricky laughed.

Oh, don't laugh.

'We could just get a big black plastic sack and fire the whole lot into it and no-one would be any the wiser.'

Oh no, Ricky thought. You couldn't pile all those nice clean clothes in with all that rubbish.

'Except the Toblerone of course. And the wine. And the clean clothes, I suppose. Oh dear, decisions, decisions.'

Creee-eeak, said the bed again. The boots moved.

'I never could make decisions. Which is why this house is so full of stuff. Can't make the decision to throw anything out. Unless it's actually stinking.'

Ricky laughed again.

'So I was just wondering, Ricky, if you would come out for a minute and help me to sort this heap of stuff.'

Ricky was thinking.

'You wouldn't have to do anything. You could just make the decisions, and I could do the actual physical part, throwing the stuff in the plastic sack or putting it wherever you suggest. And you needn't worry. Anything we can't decide about, we can just put it back on the stairs again. What d'you say?'

Ricky thought he'd better open his eyes. But when he did, he got a shock. There was an upside-down face talking, hanging over the edge of the bed. It had hair on top and hair underneath. For a moment, Ricky thought he was imagining things. Then he realised the face had a beard, a huge beard like a bush, no, like a forest. It really was Santa Claus!

'I'm Tomo, by the way,' the upside-down face was saying, the mouth where the eyes should be. 'I'm the dad around here. Except everyone calls me Tomo. No respect!'

The upside-down eyes twinkled, though. He didn't look as if he cared much for respect.

'And you must be Ricky, right?' Tomo went on.

Ricky nodded.

'C'mon so. I'll get the plastic sack. You start thinking, OK?'

You go, Froggo. You help. Come on, Froggo. Spiderboy help you to help Santy-man.

CHAPTER 5

Ricky Helps

'Why don't you talk, my bird?' Rosheen was doing her homework that evening at one end of the kitchen table, in a square of sunlight. Ricky sat at her side, watching the progress of her pen across the lined page. 'Are you afraid?'

Ricky shrugged.

'Can you not find the words?'

Ricky shrugged.

'Do you forget how?'

Ricky shrugged.

'Cat got your tongue?'

Ricky smiled, then shot his tongue out between pink lips and waggled it, to show it existed. Delightedly, Rosheen grabbed at it, but Ricky whisked it back into his mouth, safe behind his teeth, and she ended up with a handful of his face instead. She slapped each cheek playfully and went back to her work.

Ricky sharpened a pencil for her, catching the black-sprinkled shavings in his hand and putting them in the bin when he had finished. Then he tidied her pencil case for her, turning everything out onto the table and scooping the used bus tickets, sweetwrappers, twisted shapes of chewing-gum foil and more pencil shavings into his cupped palm, and making another trip to the bin. Then he placed everything back carefully, the pens and pencils lining the bottom, rubber and sharpener tucked into corners.

'Bdong, bdong, bdong,' said the radio set solemnly. 'Bdong, bdong, bdong.' A mournful sound.

'Six o'clock,' said Rosheen, zipping up her pencil case and slapping her copybook shut. 'Time to move upstairs. Mammy Kelly'll be starting tea soon. Want to come?'

Ricky clasped Froggo to him and shook his head.

'Do you not like upstairs?'

Ricky said nothing.

'Is it the dark? We can put the light on if you like.'

Ricky still said nothing.

'You're going to have to come upstairs some time, you know. You can't sleep in the living room all the time.'

Ricky looked away.

'Want to lay the table then?'

Ricky faltered.

Rosheen understood. 'Me and you, that's two. Mammy Kelly and Tomo, that's four. Fergal and Lauren, that's six.' Then she started to use her fingers. 'Charlotte, Helen, Thomas, Emma, Seamus and Billy. How many's that? Two? Can't be two. Oh, yes, twelve. Can you do twelve?'

Ricky looked doubtful.

'Do you understand twelve?'

He nodded.

'OK, look, one at each end, and five down each side.'

Ricky looked at the kitchen table. It was long, but it didn't look long enough for that.

'It'll be all right,' Rosheen assured him. 'Some of the little ones are dead thin.'

Then she raised her voice and called out: 'Ricky is going to lay the table, Mammy Kelly.' And she danced out of the bright, light, green-and-white kitchen, into the dusk of the hall and disappeared.

There was a jingle of bracelets and a swish of skirts, and Mammy Kelly appeared in the doorway.

'Knives and forks in the drawer in the middle there, Ricky. Plates on the dresser. Butter and sugar in that press over there and milk in the fridge. You'll have to open two cartons of juice. In the fridge too. Glasses in that press up there. Can you reach? If you can't there's a climbing-stool behind the back door.'

Ricky's eyes whizzed around as she talked. Drawer. Dresser. Press. Fridge. Oh! Fridge. Press. Back door. He felt breathless at the thought of remembering it all. What if he made a mistake? What if he spilt something? What if he couldn't find something? What if there weren't enough dishes? What if he dropped one and broke it? Was there a belt? Or a cane? Spiderboy doesn't like laying tables.

'Fergal's a vegetarian,' Mammy Kelly said, opening

the cutlery drawer, so Ricky could see. 'Do you know what that is?'

Ricky was counting knives. There were enough.

'He doesn't eat meat. Only cheese and fruit and bread. He doesn't like vegetables, which is a bit inconvenient for a vegetarian, isn't it?'

Ricky was counting forks. There were enough.

'Dairy though, he eats that all right. Which is something, I suppose. Protein, don't you know.'

Ricky was counting plates. There were enough. He moved them carefully to the table and started to spread them out. He didn't break any.

'Yoghurt, eggs, that sort of thing. I don't know why they call eggs "dairy", do you? I never heard of a cow that laid an egg, did you?'

Ricky was counting cups.

'Anyway, it's quiche tonight, only there's ham in it, so Fergal will have to have a boiled egg instead.'

Egg-cup, thought Ricky, and trotted back to the dresser for one.

'Good thinking, Ricky,' said Mammy Kelly.

Ricky smiled as he opened the fridge. How do you open these juice cartons?

'Scissors in the drawer,' said Mammy Kelly. 'Here, I'll do it. It's very easy to spill it if you haven't got the knack. Hope they don't all get hives. I forgot we had eggs for breakfast too. Do you get hives, Ricky? From too many eggs, I mean?'

Ricky never ate too many eggs, so he didn't know. He shook his head and then nodded it to be on the safe side.

'I see,' said Mammy Kelly. '*That* complicated. Oh dear!'

Ricky smiled again and counted everything just one more time to be sure.

CHAPTER 6

In the Attic

Ricky had gone with Rosheen without really thinking about it, after tea, and now here he was, up past the rocking-chair on the first, dark half-landing, up past the dark first floor where half the family slept, up to the second, dark half-landing, with another bathroom door, and outside it yet another bookcase, and in front of that, a large chest, with a padded lid-seat and a huge bird-mobile swaying and clanking overhead. The birds looked as if they might swoop down at any moment and swipe your eye out.

On he toiled after Rosheen, up into the dark again. He didn't like the dark and he didn't like the height. He felt as if he might go rolling back down the stairs at any minute. But he kept going, just concentrating on keeping his eyes on Rosheen's heels as they flashed from step to step ahead of him. Next came the second floor, where the other half of the family slept, high up, looking down on the treetops. Then one more flight, narrower this time, and darker, and unbroken by a half-landing. This must be the top now, the very top.

There were two rooms up here in the attic, way up at

the top of the house, hunching secretly under the roof, where no-one much slept, except extras like himself. Rosheen turned when they reached the attic floor.

'Well done, Ricky, you made it!'

She opened a door into one of the under-eaves rooms. Like every space and every available surface in this house, it was full of things. An old sewing machine, the type you have to pedal, treadle, to keep going, and heaps of brightly coloured fabric. An old-fashioned manual typewriter, still with its two-tone red-and-blue ribbon. A dressmaker's dummy wearing a huge lampshade, with a fringe, so that it looked like a naked lady at the races. A very wobbly-looking desk, piled high with boxes and piles of books. A box spilling hard and shiny bars of glass over its edges. A room full of promise. You might find anything there. Ricky stood on the threshold and stared, and sneezed.

But Rosheen closed that door and turned to the other door on the attic landing. She flung it open.

'This is your room,' she announced, standing back against the door to let him enter alone. The room was quite small, and of a very odd shape, with the ceiling sloping down on all sides, but all the same Ricky was dazzled by a sense of space and light as he stood in the doorway. Nowhere had he seen so much unoccupied space in this crazy, higgledy-piggledy, overstuffed house. The room was curiously, blessedly empty, except for a narrow iron bed and a tall and slender wardrobe. Both these items stood directly on a plain wooden floor. The walls were painted white, and there were no friezes, no pictures, no borders, no panels, no ornamentation of any sort.

He turned to Rosheen, his eyes shining. 'Yours?' he said, in a muffled tone, barely managing to get the word out.

It was the first word she had ever heard him utter.

'No, yours,' she said gently.

'Yes,' he nodded, 'yours.'

'Now, are you sure you won't mind being up here all by yourself? Fergal and Thomas and Seamus have the room directly below you. Look, your floor is their ceiling, so if you get scared in the night you can just bang on the floor and someone will come and make sure everything's OK. Now, are you sure that'll be all right? Because if you prefer, you know you can share with them, only it'll be a bit of a squeeze, but they won't mind if you don't.'

'Yes,' stuttered Ricky.

'Yes, what? Yes, it's OK or yes you'd rather share with them?'

'No,' said Ricky. 'Yes.' He shook his head and nodded it and shook and nodded it, frustrated that he couldn't express his delight with this room. He was afraid of being alone up here, of course he was, but he wasn't going to let that stop him enjoying it. 'Yes,' he said again, emphatically sitting down on the end of the bed.

Rosheen took this yes to be a yes to the room.

'OK,' she said. 'It's yours.'

'Yours,' he said with satisfaction, nodding agreeably. 'Yours.'

'No,' giggled Rosheen, 'not mine, yours.'

'Yours,' Ricky agreed, and smiled at her. He placed Froggo solemnly on the pillow and stood back to judge the effect. 'Yours,' he repeated.

CHAPTER 7

Helen Sticks the Knife In

'Why doesn't he have to go to school?' asked Helen, buttering her toast with vehemence and gesturing towards Ricky with her head. 'I mean, we all have to. What's so special about him?'

It was Ricky's second breakfast in the tall house. He was still finding mealtimes noisy and scary, but he was learning not to jump at every raised voice. As long as he didn't get in anyone's way, he figured, and as long as he stuck with Rosheen, who was clearly his friend, he'd be OK.

Thomas and Seamus were rolling up pieces of toast into tiny balls and catapulting them at each other, using their knives as launching pads. A stray toast pellet suddenly came Ricky's way, and he flailed his arms as if he was being attacked by some huge bird of prey or a deadly poison arrow. His elbow deflected the toast pellet and it fell harmlessly on the tablecloth. 'Sorry,' muttered Seamus ungraciously. Ricky grinned foolishly at him, to show it was all right, though it wasn't really. His heart was pounding, and just then another pellet hit him with a soft sting on the side of the cheek. 'Sorry,' said Thomas this time, but with a laugh in his voice. Hesitantly, Ricky gave a little laugh too, hoping he was doing the right thing. He put his hand to his face and looked wildly around, searching for clues as to how he should behave.

'Ricky's new,' said Mammy Kelly firmly to Helen, as she poured tea from a big teapot shaped like a kettle. 'I saw that, Thomas Kelly!' she said, almost in the same breath. 'If you don't stop messing with the food there'll be trouble.'

Thomas made a face but he stopped flicking toast about. Ricky gave another grin in Thomas's direction, hoping to get him on his side, but Thomas had lost interest in toast pellets and was now arm-wrestling Seamus.

There was milk in the tea already, as it was poured out of the kettle. Ricky liked his tea black, but people here seemed to assume that everyone took milk in their tea, so he was learning to drink it that way too.

'He's not *new*,' said Helen, determined to bring the conversation back to Ricky. 'He's at least nine years old, I'd say. That's not new. If he was a dress he'd be old.' And she smirked at her own cleverness, showing a row of small white teeth.

Ricky looked away, wishing they would just stop talking about him. All he wanted was to be ignored. Lauren hissed at Helen to shut her up, but Helen just went on smirking. Lauren lost interest then because at that moment Billy stood up on his chair, reached for the cornflakes packet and keeled over, right into Lauren's cereal bowl. Ricky saw him fall, like a small, plump shooting star and flung his arms out towards him, but he was too far away to save him. Billy set up a wailing and Ricky closed his ears with his fingers and briefly shut his eyes. But it was worse with his eyes closed. It all seemed even louder, somehow, and stopping his ears just made the sounds more distant, but not softer, so he unstopped them and opened his eyes again.

'Oh my God,' screamed Lauren, jumping up and flapping her school skirt. Spatters of milk came flying off it. 'I'm soaking. And look at Billy! His hair is all milk. Look, Ma, he's got cornflakes sticking to him! Oh he's such a mess! There's milk everywhere!'

Mammy Kelly was unruffled. He's new to us,' she explained to Helen, still talking about Ricky, as she stood up, picked Billy out of Lauren's breakfast, and wiped his face and fluffy little head with a J-cloth she produced apparently out of nowhere. 'And he's not a dress, you foolish child. I think you'd better change your skirt, Lauren. Wear your blue one. It's close enough to your uniform. They mightn't notice, and if they do, explain what happened.'

Billy started to whimper. He didn't like having his face wiped. Mammy Kelly sat down, put him on her knee and jostled him up and down to make him feel better.

Helen wasn't a bit pleased at the way events were distracting everyone from the conversation she wanted to

46

have. 'I know he's not a dress,' she went on determinedly. 'I didn't say he was, did I? And what makes you think you can call me a foolish child?' She'd stopped smirking by now and, looking slyly from Rosheen to Ricky to Billy, she spat out: 'You never call any of *them* names.' She meant the foster-children.

'Yes, you're right, Helen,' said Mammy Kelly wearily, still jiggling Billy and making vague daubs at him with the J-cloth.

It was always like this when somebody new came. Helen seemed to think she had to make a fuss every time, just to make sure her mother wasn't forgetting about her. As if she would!

'I'm sorry, Helen, love,' Mammy Kelly said carefully. 'I shouldn't have called you that, but really what I meant was that you were pretending to be foolish, whereas I know perfectly well that you aren't.'

Helen was mollified at this semi-compliment, but she couldn't let go: 'I was only pointing out,' she whined, 'that he's not new.'

This was too much for Mammy Kelly's patience. 'You were only being smart, Helen,' she said. 'I've explained the situation now, and I don't want to hear any more about it, OK? I won't have Ricky being discussed like this as if he wasn't here. You wouldn't like it if it was you.'

Helen opened her mouth, but before she could get a word out, her mother put a hand up, palm outwards, in the air in front of her.

'No, Helen, I don't want another word, now. You heard me. I'm serious about this. End of conversation. If you don't give over, there will be no telly for you this evening.'

Billy started to cry in earnest now, frightened by the tension he sensed in Mammy Kelly's voice.

'Shush, shush,' Mammy Kelly said, standing up and hoisting Billy onto her shoulder. 'Shush, Billykins. I didn't mean you. It's all right, lovey. Shush now.'

Helen pouted, but didn't argue further. She didn't want to miss telly. She was lucky that was the worst punishment she could imagine, but she didn't know how lucky.

'And we'll see about Ricky going to school when he's settled in, won't we, Ricky?' Mammy Kelly said, doing a little on-the-spot jig and patting Billy on the back. It seemed to be working, because Billy had stopped crying and now had his thumb in his mouth and his milk-streaked cheek rested softly next to Mammy Kelly's.

Ricky looked up at Mammy Kelly with wide eyes. He'd been to school before, of course, but he never seemed to last very long. He didn't know why. He supposed they mustn't like him in the schools, but he wasn't sure if that was it. And then they'd moved a lot, so that meant changing schools.

Changing schools was confusing. Ricky couldn't see why all the schools didn't do the same things at the same time, but they never seemed to. Every time he started at a new school, they were in the middle of something they hadn't done in his last school, and he couldn't work out what was going on, because he'd missed out on the beginning. And then as soon as he began to get the hang of fractions or decimals or whatever it was, they'd suddenly go on to something else, and it would always be something he'd done six months ago somewhere else. He'd done the same three stories in his English reader four times in four different schools, but he never seemed to catch up on the other stories. And he had done long division at least twice, but it took him ages to get the hang of it, because he didn't seem ever to have done ordinary division to start with. Once he worked that out, he was flying, but nobody had noticed he hadn't learnt it, so he'd had to teach himself. School was not Ricky's idea of a good place to go.

'It's OK, Ricky. It needn't be for a while yet,' said Mammy Kelly, noticing the look of panic on his small white face, 'not till you're good and ready. You can stay home with me and Tomo and Billy for a while. That'll be nice, Billy, won't it?'

'Huh!' Helen couldn't suppress a snort, though she didn't dare say anything.

Rosheen nudged Ricky's ankle under the table and when he looked at her to see what she wanted, she mouthed something at him and jabbed her finger in Helen's direction. Helen was sitting next to her, opposite Ricky. Ricky frowned. He couldn't make out what Rosheen was trying to tell him, though he thought she must be warning him about something. She mouthed again, and jabbed her finger more fiercely, but still Ricky couldn't work it out. He screwed up his eyes in concentration, trying to read her lips, when suddenly her mouth went into a wide, wide O and he could see her bottom teeth. Her tongue tipped the roof of her mouth in an effort to prevent herself yelping. In spite of herself, she let out a little squeaking sound, but nobody heard except Ricky.

Somebody had kicked or pinched her. It must have been Helen, but she was calmly and innocently talking to Seamus about football. Ricky looked at Rosheen again. She had closed her mouth now, and her lips were smacked together in a grimace. Ricky raised his eyebrows in Helen's direction, and Rosheen nodded, but then she shook her head to indicate that she wasn't going to tell. And then, quick as a flash, she dug her bony elbow hard into Helen's ribs.

Now it was Helen's turn to give a squeak of pain and surprise. Rosheen smiled sweetly at her and pushed the marmalade towards her. Helen looked daggers at her, dug her knife viciously into the pot and twisted it savagely in the marmalade. She looked as if she meant business.

'And there'll be muffins for tea, Helen,' said Mammy Kelly, noting her daughter's angry jabbing movements and trying to distract her. 'I'm going to bake them this afternoon, so they'll be lovely and fresh.'

'Mm,' said Helen, who loved her food, but she couldn't find it in herself to say thank you.

CHAPTER 8

The Pigeons

The back garden of the tall house sloped away up from the back door. Outside the back door was a small yard, for the bins and bikes, with the remains of a herb garden Mammy Kelly had once tried to grow in a big pot, the kind with pockets for trailing things to grow out of. All that was left was a very straggly lavender bush with a few greyish leaves near the tips. All the other herbs had died.

Then there were steps, very steep ones, like the ones at the front of the house going up from the gate, only steeper still. The steps were carved out of a brambly waste that never had had much chance to be a garden. The grain bucket banged against Ricky's knees every time he took a step up. He was following Rosheen, who was carrying a jug of water with a long spout.

And at the top of the steps was a long low shed. This was where the pigeons lived. They were supposed to be Tomo's pigeons, Rosheen had explained. He used to race pigeons at one stage, but now they were just pets, and Rosheen was in charge of feeding them.

It was darkish inside the shed, because the windows

were small and grimy, and it smelt warm and bitter at the same time. The pigeons made soft throaty sounds to each other and rustled their wings and fussed when the door opened. Flap-flap, they fussed, who's this, now, friend or foe? Only Rosheen, but oh-oh-oh, boh-boh-botheration, she has a boy with her, su-uu-ure to be trouble, flap-flap. They turned their heads away and looked over their shoulders as if there was someone behind them, but there wasn't.

'You feed them,' whispered Rosheen to Ricky. 'That way they'll know you're a friend.'

Ricky looked around, blinking in the grey light of the pigeon shed. Rosheen nudged him in the direction of the feeding troughs, pointing them out to him. The ground was soft and soundless beneath his feet, all sawdust and feathers. He lifted the bucket and gently spilt the grain into the containers with a soughing sound like dry rain, moving the bucket along as each container filled.

The pigeons watched him, burbling questioningly to each other as he worked, but they kept to their perches until he had finished. Then one came fluttering down to investigate. Then another, and another, and soon the whole flock had descended and was flustering and flittering about the feeding dishes, making little dashes with their beaks and nabbing grains.

'Watch this,' said Rosheen softly, and she dug into the almost empty bucket. She gathered the remaining few grains from the bottom and then held out her hand, slightly cupped, with the grains in the shallow dent she had made of her palm. One of the smallest birds, a creamy white pigeon with brownish-streaked wings, who had been flapping anxiously about the edge of the flock trying to get a beak in, saw what she was doing and took off with a flurry from the feeding-frenzied crowd. It landed perkily on Rosheen's wrist. It stopped for a moment to get a good grip with its longest claw and then bent its head into Rosheen's hand and picked a grain. It swallowed quickly and took a beady-eyed look around, before dipping its head once again and taking another grain. When it had finished dipping and swallowing, it turned to look Rosheen in the eye, and then flew back up to its perch and sat there watching its companions and occasionally investigating its feathery chest.

'His name is Fudge,' Rosheen whispered. 'You can do that next time. You just have to learn to keep still, even when it tickles.'

Ricky nodded vigorously, his eyes shining. He had never experienced anything like those birds – the soft, sudden whickering of their wings as they took off on short, impetuous, feathery flights and the querying warbling of their voices as they jostled and nudged each other on their perches, all in the warm and muffled air of their low, dry, padded house.

'I have to go now,' said Rosheen. 'Homework to finish. Will you just fill up their water dishes, and make sure you bolt the door after you.'

Ricky started to fill the water dishes from the long-spouted jug. He hardly noticed Rosheen leaving the pigeon shed. Then he stood still for a long time and just watched the birds, listening to their murmelings. He didn't know how long he stayed there in the warm, pigeony gloom. Presently, he heard a sound outside. Perhaps it was Rosheen coming back, to call him in for his tea maybe. He thought he'd been about ten minutes with the birds, but it might have been much longer. He'd better go.

He reached out his hand, not daring to touch a bird, but wanting to make a gesture to them, to tell them how wonderful he thought them. The birds huddled together and settled themselves, smoothing their fronts with their beaks, butting their shoulders with their cheeks, folding themselves into themselves and puffing and ruffling their feathery duvet-coats. As Ricky raised his hand, a ripple went through the burbling, billowing, shuffling company, as if the whole colony was acknowledging Ricky's salute. Good night, goo-ooo-ood night. Ahhh! Good night.

CHAPTER 9

The Blockade

When he came out into the evening light after the shadowy shed, Ricky was blinded. He could hear Rosheen and just make out her shape coming fuzzily up the steps, but he couldn't really see her with his eyes crinkled up against the sun. He blinked a few times and concentrated on seeing her.

It wasn't Rosheen after all. It was that other one, the one with shiny, putty-coloured skin stretched over her nose. Helen.

Helen was quite close now, close enough to touch. She stood stock still and stared at Ricky. She had a bunched-up plastic bag in her hand, which she carried at an awkward angle. It creaked and rustled a lot, as if it was alive.

Ricky smiled and transferred the jug to the same hand as the bucket. That gave him a free hand to put over his eyes to create a sun shade so he could see Helen better, but still all he could really see was the shape of her body and the flossy outline of her hair against the sunlight. Her face was a mess of shadows.

He stepped forward, sidling to edge past Helen, but Helen didn't sidle to the opposite side of the step. She stood her ground. In fact she moved her feet so that Ricky couldn't get past her without stepping on her toes. There was nothing for it but to shuffle off the step and onto the steeply sloping bramble-covered earth, so Ricky did that, sidling again to keep as close as possible to the steps and not get snarled in the brambles. Helen moved her feet again, stomping one shoe right in front of Ricky's, crushing a scraggy bramble bush. Ricky moved edgeways, farther from the steps and into the brambly wilderness, feeling his ankles being scratched, but Helen was ahead of him, her foot again blocking his way. Reddening slightly, Ricky tried going back towards the steps, but Helen's other foot stomped down in front of him again. They were like two people meeting in a narrow doorway and bobbing about politely, each trying to let the other through, only it wasn't politeness – Helen was deliberately blocking Ricky's way.

'Excuse me,' she said to Ricky then.

Ricky put up his hand to acknowledge her words and to accept her apology.

But Helen wasn't apologising.

'Excuse me,' she repeated. 'It's what you say when you want to get past somebody on a narrow path.'

Ricky nodded frantically, desperate to humour her.

'Well then, say it,' said Helen, firmly setting her foot right in front of Ricky's feet.

Ricky nodded again and waved.

'Say it!' hissed Helen, her face pressed very close to Ricky's now, their noses almost touching.

Ricky opened his mouth, but no sound came out.

'Excuse me,' said Helen, her breath on his face. 'It's not so difficult. Just two little words. Come on. You have to learn your manners, you know.'

He hasta learn manners, Nancy, I keep telling you, it's for his own good. I'll put manners on him, so I will. Kids have no manners these days, but I was brought up to have manners to my betters, and he will too, if I have to beat it into him.

If!

Suddenly Ricky let fly with the bucket and jug and hit Helen a clattering wallop on the hip. She gasped, more in surprise than pain, and stepped back, holding her side. 'You hit me!' she shouted in outrage. 'You hit me! I never touched you and you hit me!'

The back door opened with a wham and Mammy Kelly came rushing up the steep steps.

'What's wrong now?' she asked, looking from Ricky to Helen and back to Ricky.

Helen was crying. Ricky was dry-eyed, but his chest was heaving.

'He hit me, Ma, that new boy. With the bucket! I think he's broken my hip-bone.'

'Don't be ridiculous,' said Mammy Kelly, but she

peered all the same at the reddened skin that Helen was exposing by turning down the waistband of her jeans. She gave Helen's hip a soothing little pat and tucked her shirt in. 'You'll be better before you're twice married,' she said.

'Huh!' said Helen. She was still holding the lumpy plastic bag in her other hand. Ricky wondered vaguely what was in it. It crackled as if something inside it was moving.

'Did you hit her, Ricky?' Mammy Kelly asked then.

Ricky nodded miserably, the bucket still swinging from his hand.

'I never touched him, Ma,' snivelled Helen. 'I swear I didn't.'

Mammy Kelly cupped Ricky's chin in her hand and asked quietly, 'Did she touch you?'

Ricky shook his head.

'Well, what did you say to him then?' asked Mammy Kelly, turning to Helen in exasperation.

'I only told him to say excuse me if he wanted to pass me on the steps,' said Helen self-righteously.

'Oh Helen! You can be so mean-minded, sometimes,' said Mammy Kelly, not looking at Helen, but at Ricky. She said it almost as if Helen wasn't there. Poor Helen, she was thinking. Can't cope with the least threat. Not even a poor little scrap like Ricky.

'Well,' whined Helen, 'he started it.'

'I have no doubt in the wide world that he didn't,' said Mammy Kelly.

'You can't prove that!' said Helen indignantly. 'How can you possibly prove it?'

'It isn't a question of proof,' said Mammy Kelly. 'Go on inside, the pair of you, and no muffins for either of you, just bread-and-butter with your tea.'

'But he started it, Ma, and he hit me!' Helen started whining again.

'If I hear another word about it, Helen,' said Mammy Kelly with sudden briskness, 'there'll be no tea at all for you.'

'You can't do that,' said Helen. 'I have to get my tea. That's child abuse.'

'Child abuse!' snorted Mammy Kelly. 'Oh, Helen, you haven't the first clue about child abuse, you lucky, lucky girl.'

She raised her arms, as if she was going to hug Helen, but Helen stepped back, so instead, Mammy Kelly just gave her a little nudge with her elbow.

'Now you're pushing me,' said Helen. 'It's not fair. That really is child abuse.'

'Give over, Helen, please,' said Mammy Kelly wearily. She reached out and took the bucket from Ricky, and as she did so, she laid a hand on his shoulder and gave it a friendly squeeze. She had a big warm buttery smile. Ricky tried to give a little smile back, but it was all he could do to keep his mouth from going crooked. Then she took the jug from Ricky as well, and said softly to him, 'Go on inside, now, Ricky, like a good boy. And don't hit anyone again, no matter how badly you want to. That doesn't solve anything, OK?'

Ricky nodded. Then, slowly, dragging his feet, he followed Helen, who was holding her rustling plastic bag awkwardly in front of her, into the house.

CHAPTER 10

The Moon Chair

'I'm going to tell your social worker you hit me,' Helen whispered in Ricky's ear as they jostled into the house together. 'You're not allowed to hit people, you know. She'll take you away from here. Probably put you in a home, or one of those places for juvenile delinquents. That's what you are, you know, a juvenile delinquent. We've had them here before, but we don't keep them if they're violent. Mammy Kelly is dead set against violence.'

Ricky put his hands over his ears. He didn't want to hear any more of what Helen had to say. He closed his eyes as well, and so he didn't notice that Helen had slipped away and was tearing up the stairs, giggling softly to herself, her plastic bag crackling and squirming in her hand. He sat for a while on a chair in the hall and listened to the sounds of the tall, tall house. The grandfather clock made a whirring sound, getting ready to chime, but then it changed its mind and just gave a polite little cough instead. It was a very old grandfather clock, which only chimed erratically and always gave the wrong time anyway. Ricky could hear the voices of children squabbling in the kitchen and the sounds of a radio playing somewhere.

Suddenly a door flew open, and the pleasant babble of children squabbling and laughing grew suddenly to a roar. Not waiting to find out whether anyone was going to come out of the opened door, Ricky fled up the stairs, two at a time. He couldn't face them all just now. He would just go up to his room for a while.

After he got to the first half-landing, the one with the rocking-chair on it, he slowed down, and for the rest of the climb he went a step at a time, his limbs suddenly weary. Up the next flight he went, past Rosheen's room, up to the second half-landing, where the big birds whooshed and spun overhead, up another flight again, past more bedrooms, and then up the final flight to the attic storey, where Ricky lived alone. He was looking forward to getting to his own room, where it was cool and quiet, where there was no clutter of books and things, where there was no Helen to tease and bully him.

He would lie on his bed for a little while and maybe have a nap. He wasn't very hungry. He'd skip tea and go back down again later, maybe watch some television. He liked watching television, because he could sit in the dark with the others and nobody put any pressure on him to make conversation. Mealtimes were more difficult.

Ricky's hand closed over the brass doorknob of his bedroom door. He turned it carefully, but the door didn't give. He pushed with his shoulder against it. Still it didn't give. It must be stuck, he thought. He pushed again. This time he brought all his strength to bear on the task, but still the door didn't move. Ricky panicked. What was wrong with his door? He flung his body at it, he kicked it, kicked it again, pushed and heaved with his shoulder, but the door stood solid against him. It must be locked.

Ricky leaned against the door, huddled up against it. He could feel tears starting in his eyes. Helen was right. There was no place for him here. Nobody wanted him. They were trying to push him out. Somebody had locked him out of his own bedroom. Ricky slithered to the floor, and sat huddled miserably against the door, every now and then listlessly banging his head against the solid wood.

Inside Ricky's room, behind the locked door, Helen stuffed her head into Ricky's pillow, trying to keep from laughing. She mustn't laugh. She mustn't make a sound or he would know she was there. She was pleased with herself that she had been clever enough to lock the door. Otherwise he'd have come bursting in and found her and then the trick would have flopped. Every time she thought about the trick, a fresh wave of giggles came surging up from her stomach and shook her body, but she didn't let a sound escape, just shook silently with laughter. Him and his stupid frog toy!

She could hear the occasional thud of Ricky's head against the door. What a stupid boy he was! Didn't he know he could hurt himself doing that? Oh well, she'd soon teach him how stupid he was. A toy frog indeed! At his age! She wondered how much longer he'd sit out there. She was starting to get hungry.

After a while, Ricky felt cold. He didn't have a jumper. His jumper was in his room, on the other side of the door that refused to budge. The more he thought about his jumper inside his bedroom, the colder he felt. He wished he had a blanket. He wished he had a pillow. He wanted to sleep. He was tired. But there was nowhere comfortable to sleep on the cold, dark, attic landing.

He sat a little longer, thinking about jumpers and blankets and pillows, and then it came to him. He thought he had seen things that looked like blankets or cloths in the other attic room, the one that Rosheen had shown him that first day she had brought him up here. Yes, he was sure he had. There'd been a big old wicker basket and it was full of something warm – blankets, quilts, sheets, something like that.

He stood up and tried the other door. It opened easily, letting out a flood of warmth and light. Whoever had locked Ricky's door hadn't thought of locking him out of this room too. The window must face the sunshine, he thought, for the room was bathed in pinkish sunset light and it was warm still from the day's sunshine. Ricky stepped gratefully into the warmth. All the objects piled higgledy-piggledy every which way in the room had been sunbathing all day, and now they basked in the evening light and seemed to give off a heat of their own. The air was stuffy and fusty and full of unspoken promises.

Helen heard Ricky moving away from the door, and she heard the sound of the other door opening and then closing. He must have gone into the room next door. Good! She'd just wait a little longer, to make sure he wasn't going to come out of that room again, and then she'd make her getaway.

Ricky had remembered right. There was a big old laundry basket with its lid pushed up by its overflowing contents. Piled-up pillows nosed comfortably out of the top and an eiderdown poured out of one corner. He'd definitely be able to make himself comfortable here, if he could just make his way through all the piled-up things to that basket in the corner.

Ricky looked around for somewhere to curl up. There wasn't much lying-down space. Perhaps he could find a spot under the big table that took up the middle of the floor. He ducked down to look. Boxes were piled up under the table, but if he moved a few maybe he could make himself a space. Hunkering down, Ricky started to push at the heavy boxes. He managed to carve out a small space and raised a cloud of dust in the process. Suddenly he was seized by a sneezing fit and rested back on his heels until it passed. There wasn't enough room yet, he thought, but he was tired. Maybe if he climbed over the table he could get at some of the boxes from a better angle and make a little more room.

He climbed onto the table and stood up, keeping an unsteady footing between towering piles of books, an old typewriter and a sewing machine. He was trying to find a place to land on the other side of the table, but there didn't seem to be much floor space. There was a brightly coloured crocheted rug flung over something tall and spiky that was pressed against the other side of the table. Maybe he could use that to wrap around himself instead of the eiderdown in the laundry basket. From his perch up on the table, Ricky pulled at the rainbow blanket. It was catching on something, so he leaned forward and used both hands to ease the loosely woven fabric over whatever it was draped on.

It was a chair. Under the multicoloured blanket was a beautiful chair with a high pointy back, almost like a chair you might see in a cathedral, a ceremonial chair of some sort. The smooth, honey-coloured back of the chair soared up to a point, and balanced right on top, looking almost as if it was growing out of the chair, was a half-moon with a smiling face in it. Ricky gasped. He had never seen anything so magical as the moon chair. He reached out and touched the moon lightly. It was smooth and warm. He stroked it. The wood was silky, and all the little nobbles and crevices were like butterscotch under his fingers.

Ricky wriggled his way off the table and slithered onto the seat of the chair. It was the most comfortable chair he had ever sat in, seeming to hold his body in its caress. Pulling the crocheted blanket right over him, Ricky lay back in the chair and closed his eyes.

Spiderboy can sit here. This blanket, all squares, all colours, wrap Spiderboy up, curl up here Froggo on this moon chair. Warm enough, Froggo? Oh yes, warm and comfy, Froggo and Spiderboy, no bully girl. Just sit still now, Froggo, nobody knows, just sit still, close eyes now at last, sun going down now, eyes tickling, dust and sunshine, just sit here now, just still and quiet, no sound, in moon chair.

Helen kept still for a long time, until she was sure Ricky wasn't coming back to try his own door again. Then very carefully she tiptoed to the door, turned the key quietly and eased it out of the lock. Then she opened the door gently, and slipped out. She closed the door carefully and then stood on tiptoe to put the key back in its place on the shelf of the lintel over the door. Then she pattered softly down the stairs.

Nobody saw her. Nobody heard her. She was safe.

CHAPTER 11

A Practical Joke

It was Rosheen who noticed Ricky wasn't at tea.

'Where's Ricky, Mammy Kelly?' she asked. 'Is he still out with the pigeons?'

'No, no,' said Mammy Kelly. 'He came in a while ago, with Helen.'

'Helen!'

'Yes, Helen was out at the shed with him.'

'But Helen hates the pigeons. She says they're smelly.'

'They are too,' said Helen, coming into the kitchen and shaking her hands in front of her. 'The towel's missing from the downstairs loo again,' she added accusingly to her mother.

'Where's Ricky?' Rosheen asked.

'I don't know,' shrugged Helen. 'I'm not his minder, am I?'

'He doesn't need a minder,' Rosheen retorted.

'It looks like he does, if he's got lost between the back door and the kitchen. I smell muffins. Oh goody!'

'No muffins for you, Helen,' said Mammy Kelly

firmly. 'You heard me.'

Helen started to argue, but Rosheen wasn't interested in hearing her.

'Excuse me,' she muttered to nobody in particular – nobody heard her anyway – and slipped down from her chair and went to look for Ricky.

Of course the first place she thought of was his bedroom in the attic, so she chased up the stairs, two at a time, calling his name as she went. By the time she got to the second half-landing, the one with the bird-mobile on it, she was beginning to get out of breath, so she stopped calling, but went on climbing.

It was quite dark on the attic landing, though it was not yet night. It was just that there was no window up here, and the bulb in the electric light had blown and nobody had bothered to fix it, because it was so high up and difficult to reach. Rosheen stood outside Ricky's door and called out softly: 'Ricky, it's me, Rosheen. Can I come in?'

No reply.

Rosheen tapped lightly on the door this time. 'Ricky,' she called, through the keyhole, 'come on, it's only me.'

Still no reply.

'Oh Ricky!' Rosheen said in a pleading voice, her mouth to the crack at the side of the door. 'Come on, you can open up for me. None of the others are with me. I won't tell anyone you're here if you don't want me to. Just open the door, come on.'

Complete silence from Ricky's bedroom. Perhaps he

was asleep? Maybe she should knock a bit harder.

Rap-rap-rap, Rosheen knocked. The silence was eerie. Maybe he wasn't there after all.

Frustrated and irritated, Rosheen turned the handle of the door. The lock clicked as it gave, and Rosheen pushed the door open just a crack, giving Ricky, if he was inside, plenty of notice that she was coming in. 'Ricky?' she called, leaning against the opening door. 'Ricky, are you there?'

Still there was no reply, so Rosheen pushed harder and the door opened with a slow screech into silent darkness. Rosheen reached for the light switch. The curtains were closed, which explained the dark, and the bed lay neatly made. Suspiciously neatly. Surely Ricky wasn't that good at bed making? Rosheen stepped across the room and flicked the covers back. It was an old-fashioned bed with blankets and sheets, not a duvet.

'Waa-aah!' Rosheen started back as a large brown frog leapt out at her, as soon as she lifted the sheet, and landed on the floor at her feet.

'Tribb-err!' said the frog, rather surprisingly, like an elderly man who smoked too much clearing his throat. 'Tribb-err, tribber!' It seemed a bit dazed, but then it pulled itself together and with two more leaps it bounded over Rosheen's rigid feet and out the door onto the landing, where Rosheen could no longer see it.

'Tribb-err, tribb-err!' she heard it say again, and then she heard a flunking noise as the frog took another leap.

Flunkety-flunk, it went, flunkety-flunk, down the stairs.

Shaking a little from the shock she'd got, Rosheen slid to the floor and sat there with her arms around her knees. From her vantage point on the floor, she could see a plastic bag crumpled up and thrown under Ricky's bed. She wondered what it was doing there, the only thing out of place in Ricky's tidy room. Who could have put the frog in Ricky's bed? she wondered. She didn't think it could have been Ricky himself. He might, she supposed, have had some confused idea that the frog would like it in his warm dry bed, but she didn't think so. Ricky would know that frogs like cool damp places. He mightn't say much, but he wasn't stupid. No, it had to have been put in Ricky's bed as a nasty practical joke. How mean!

Poor old frog, Rosheen thought. She stood up, brushed herself down and folded the plastic bag without thinking much about what she was doing. She put the folded plastic bag on the bed and went looking for the frog.

Rosheen found the frog on one of the half-landings, cowering under a chair. She picked it up and took it downstairs and out into the back garden, where she left it in the shade of a large mossy stone.

CHAPTER 12

Ricky Goes Moon-flying

Oh Froggo, look! It's great here, I think we must be on the moon, it's all shiny, look it's bright and light, there's oh! there's a rainbow, only it's not a rainbow, it's filling the whole sky, the whole sky is a rainbow, it's like a roof, like a roof made of rainbow, all glittering with stars. A rainbow with stars! And, hey! I'm not walking under the rainbow, I'm flying, I'm gliding, I'm floating. Wheee! It's oh, it's like, what is it like, Froggo? I don't know, do you? It's like sailing, only it's in the air, it's air-sailing! It's like being a bird. Do you think the pigeons fly like this, Froggo? Oh yes, look, there's that pigeon, the one with the browny wings, yes, yes, it's the one Rosheen fed from her hand. Fudge it's called, it's flying along with us, Froggo, it's smiling at me! Oh look at its wings, all spread out like sails, look it's got browny streaks on its wings on top, but here underneath, where the softest feathers are, it's all white, white, white, white like snow, all soft and feathery-white like snow, only not cold, not cold at all, warm and feathery-white. You could sleep under the pigeon's wings, you could just nestle right in there and sleep. Do you think you could sleep and fly at the same time, Froggo? Sleep-flying that would be. And the air, it's sweet and it's cool and warm at the same time, it's cool without being cold and warm without being hot, it's just perfect, it's like water only it's not wet. We can whoop down too, and then whoosh back up again. You don't just have to glide along, you can whirl about and go on your back, like the back stroke, and you can do a swoop and a swing and you can dip off to one side and then straighten up and glide again if you want to, oh! it's so wonderful. And there's music too, Froggo. Can you hear it? No, it's voices, nice voice. Froggo, Froggo, I think I hear Rosheen's voice. I do, I do, I hear her. She's calling me, she's saying Ricky, Ricky, let me in!

CHAPTER 13

'You Are the Moon King'

After leaving the frog outdoors, Rosheen came back into the house and trudged up the stairs again, to re-make Ricky's bed. She didn't want him to know anything about the frog episode, but if she left the sheet turned down and the plastic bag on the bed he'd know something odd had happened. Poor old Ricky. It wasn't fair to tease him like that. He was shy and scared enough as it was, without putting a frog in his bed.

She didn't know for sure who had put the frog in Ricky's bed, but she had a shrewd idea it must have been Helen – she'd been picking on Ricky since he'd arrived. What had got into that girl? Rosheen wondered. Why was she so determined to make Ricky miserable? But there was no point in confronting her with it. She'd only deny it and then there'd be a row and probably Rosheen would end up in trouble instead of Helen. Rosheen sighed.

'Ricky!' she called, when she reached Ricky's room, rattling the door handle hopelessly and rapping on the door again, though she knew he wasn't there. No reply came, so Rosheen creaked the bedroom door open once again, and had a good look around. Nothing had changed. The bed clothes were still pulled back, as she'd left them after the frog jumped out at her. She went in and gave the bed a good tweaking and smoothed it over again. There! You'd never guess, she thought.

Then something occurred to her. She left the light on in Ricky's room and the door open, so that there was some light on the gloomy landing, and she went and rattled the door of the other attic room.

'Ricky!' she called again, and opened the door. The light from Ricky's room revealed a lot of humpy shapes in the other room. Rosheen reached out and felt for the light switch.

'Ricky?' she called as the light came on, her eyes travelling around the room: sewing machine, dressmaker's dummy, bolts of cloth, baskets full of patchwork pieces and knitting wool, a large basket of pillows and quilts, a desk, a chair, a box full of pieces of glass. A chair with a brightly coloured blanket screwed up in a strange shape on it. A blanket that breathed! She'd found him!

'Ricky!' Rosheen shook Ricky's shoulder and pulled the blanket down to reveal his sleepy-eyed face. 'You idiot. How could you sleep with your face all muffled up like that! You could have suffocated.'

Ricky blinked at her, shading his eyes from the light. He had Froggo in one hand as usual.

'Rosheen!' he said with a smile.

'Yes!' cried Rosheen delightedly, 'that's right, it's me, Rosheen.' He'd never spoken her name before. 'It's Rosheen,' she repeated, idiotic with pleasure.

'Rosheen,' Ricky said again, with a smile, delighted to be able to please her.

'Oh Ricky!' Rosheen said then, 'what a lovely chair! Where did you find it? Was it always here? I never saw it before. Oh look, it's a moon chair! It's like, like, like a throne. Oh Ricky, it's a throne for the moon king!'

Ricky smiled happily and yawned.

'You must be the moon king, Ricky,' Rosheen said.

Ricky smiled some more.

'Yes, that's it, that's it!' Rosheen cried. 'You are the moon king!'

'Moon?' said Ricky experimentally.

'Yes, yes, Ricky.' Rosheen was thrilled. He was starting to talk, and it was to her that he talked. He must really trust her. 'You are the moon king, Ricky,' she said again. 'You are the moon king.'

'You – are – the – moon – king,' Ricky said carefully after her.

'No, no, Ricky, you always get that wrong. I can't be a moon king, I'm a girl. I can be a queen, but not a king. *You* are the moon king.'

'You are the moon king,' Ricky repeated.

'No, no, oh Ricky, can't you get this right? Listen. Say it after me: "I am the moon king."'

'I?' said Ricky.

'Yes, yes, "I", that's right,' said Rosheen. '"I am the moon king."'

'You are the moon king!' said Ricky again. 'You are the moon king!'

'No, Ricky, you've still got it wrong. You are the moon king!'

'You are the moon king!' said Ricky happily. 'You are the moon king.'

CHAPTER 14

Mowing the Lawn

Tomo came lumbering in the back door one afternoon, pulling and hauling at a large, cumbersome and foul-smelling lawnmower. Ricky was sitting at the kitchen table, painting a picture of Rosheen.

Nobody had mentioned school since that day a few weeks ago when Helen had asked at breakfast why Ricky wasn't going. Ricky hoped they wouldn't bring it up again. He didn't want to face into school yet. The only bit he'd ever really enjoyed in school was art, and they'd only done art once a week in any school he'd been in. Anyway, he wasn't ready for school yet. He was just settling in with the Kellys and starting to enjoy being there. He missed his mother, but life had been so complicated at home recently, with Ed there and everything, that he didn't want to go back there, or not for now anyway. He was starting to feel safe here.

In Ricky's picture, Rosheen was dancing. She was like a dandelion flower. Her yellow dress was all puffed out with air from the dance and her hair was yellow and streaming out like moonbeams, like that first night when she knocked on his door because she thought he was a banshee.

'There y'are.' Tomo nodded at Ricky.

Tomo was often at home during the day. He did shiftwork and his hours were constantly changing. He wasn't good at adjusting his sleeping patterns to fit with his shifts, though, so he was often up and mooching about the house when he should really have been catching up on his sleep. That's what he was at today.

Ricky noticed that Tomo's face was bright pink from the exertion of managing the lawnmower, which looked as heavy and awkward as it was smelly and ungainly. He took a big blue hanky out of his pocket and mopped his face. Ricky had never seen anyone do that before, only heard about it in books. Policemen did it in stories and station-masters and firemen, large people in heavy clothes. He looked tired, Ricky thought, tired and overworked. He looked like he needed a hand.

Ricky didn't want to stop painting. He had just got the yellow for Rosheen's hair right, and he'd had to mix and mix to get it like that. He didn't want the paint to go all hard now. But …

Ricky looked thoughtfully at Tomo and the lawnmower for a moment. Then he wiped his paintbrush carefully on the sheets of newspaper Mammy Kelly had spread on the table, to get the paint off it, and dropped it into his jamjar of water. He put the lids back on all the paints. Then he wiped his painty hands on the damp J-cloth

Mammy Kelly had given him and slithered off the chair.

He went and stood beside Tomo and waited for him to stop wiping the perspiration off his face. Tomo finally bunched the blue hanky up and crammed it back into his pocket. Then he noticed Ricky standing there.

'Are you right, so?' said Tomo, as if he had been expecting Ricky all along to help him with the lawnmower.

Right, Ricky nodded.

'Good lad,' said Tomo. 'The kitchen isn't too bad. Rough old floor, you know.'

The lawnmower kept catching wilfully in things and being cussed, but eventually they got it as far as the door out of the kitchen.

'Now comes the hard part,' said Tomo.

The hard part! thought Ricky, already hot and panting with the effort of moving the lawnmower.

'We have to get it through this door, and then take it through the house without doing any damage. That means we can't push it along the floor, because it might scratch things, you know, catch in things, scuff things, get caught up in the rugs, bash into the doorposts. So you see, we have to sort of lift it through the house.'

Sort of lift it!

'Now, I'm biggish, so I'll take the weight of it. You just hold it up so I don't drop it, OK?'

OK, Ricky nodded.

Walking through a house backwards tilting up a

heavy, awkward, smelly lawnmower is not easy, even if the other person is taking most of the weight. Ricky was worn out when they finally reached the front porch with their burden, but he wasn't finished yet.

Tomo lunged with the lawnmower off the porch and onto the front lawn and hung, exhausted, perspiration gathering in little streams down his face and into his beard, over the handle.

'Now, I'll get the petrol, and then we'll get started.'

Petrol. So that was what the unpleasant smell was. Ricky didn't know lawnmowers ran on petrol. His nana's lawnmower was a dinky little green thing that you just pushed and it made a nice satisfying sound like a corncrake and grass cuttings came flying out of it. It was like a little factory, whirring and crunching and producing lots of sweet-smelling grass, like toy hay, which you had to rake up at the end.

Tomo had disappeared into the house, and now he reappeared carrying a dirt-streaked plastic bottle with a filthy rag around the lid. He poured the petrol into the lawnmower, re-plugged the bottle and then he started to pull at a special string thing that was part of the lawnmower. Every time he pulled, the lawnmower screamed, and then stopped. Pull, scream, silence; pull, scream, silence. It didn't want to go.

'Here, you try,' said Tomo.

So Ricky pulled. But this time, the lawnmower didn't even scream. It just sort of sobbed and jerked a bit and then went silent. Ricky tried again. This time, he couldn't even get the string out of its little container. His nostrils were full of the smell of petrol and his hands were smeared with oil and dirt and he was tired. He tried the string one more time, and the lawnmower gave a little phutting sound and died again. Ricky plonked down on the lawn and put his head in his hands. When he opened his eyes, he could see the lawn all around him, like a green sea. The grass didn't look long to him. He couldn't understand why Tomo thought it needed to be cut.

'Here, don't sit there,' said Tomo. 'How am I going to mow the lawn if you are sitting in the middle of it like a garden gnome?'

Ricky crawled to the path and lay on it, flat on his back, looking up at the sky. There were tiny little clouds in it, little puffball things, miles high, and the sky was much vaster when you looked at it from flat on your back. The earth shook then, as Tomo finally yanked the lawnmower into life, and started to mow the lawn, up and down, up and down, screaming and whining. Ricky could hear it right in his ears, as if the lawnmower was screaming at him. Like the sky, the lawnmower's voice seemed much bigger when he was lying on the ground, so he pulled himself up into a sitting position, and sure enough the whine of the lawnmower got instantly less and the sky seemed immediately less far away and endless.

Tomo didn't need help now, so Ricky sat on the path and chewed a stem of grass and just watched him. The front lawn sloped steeply to the gate, and Tomo had a job keeping the lawnmower from flying away from him, off down the slope and into the laurel hedge at the bottom of the garden. He was like somebody walking a very large and energetic dog.

A thought occurred to Ricky, and he stood up and bounded into the house, through to the back door, up the back garden to the shed where the lawnmower lived, next to the pigeons. Yes, sure enough, there was a garden rake. One or two teeth were missing, and it was heavy, but he could manage it. He carried it gingerly through the house, sidling it through the doors so that it didn't snag, and out into the sunny front garden again. Then he started to rake the area of lawn that Tomo had mown. When Tomo turned around at the end of a stretch he waved to Ricky over the throb and whine of the lawnmower and gave him a thumbs-up. Ricky waved back and went on raking.

When the lawn was all done, Tomo brought two tall glasses of lemonade out of the house and they both sat on a garden bench holding the icy glasses in their hands and surveying their work.

It was home-made lemonade. Ricky didn't usually like drinks with bits in and no fizz, but he was so hot and so thirsty from his work that he gulped it down in long, cold and deliciously sharp-tasting draughts.

'Thanks, son,' said Tomo, raising his lemonade glass.

Ricky raised his glass back. You're welcome, he smiled.

CHAPTER 15

The Ruined Picture

Indoors was cool and dark after the bright warmth of the garden. Ricky's limbs felt heavy from exertion and the sun, and coloured shapes, after-images of the sun, swam in front of his eyes as he entered the hall. Even after blinking he could hardly see, and he staggered forward to the kitchen, flailing his rubbery arms in front of him.

He was still having trouble adjusting his vision when he reached the light-filled kitchen. Shapes floated in the air like oily blobs on water and he had to blink hard several times. Gradually the room assembled itself in front of him, and he could make out the table, as he had left it, covered in newspapers and his painting things. But what had happened to his picture? He'd left it drying on the table, but it wasn't there now, just a … Oh no! It was there, but not opened out flat to dry. Somebody had folded it over. Now it was going to be all stuck together, if the paint hadn't been allowed to dry first.

Gingerly, Ricky picked up the folded sheet and started to prise it open, very gently and carefully. It had stuck, quite badly, but he managed to open it without tearing it at least. The two halves eased themselves apart with sticky resistance.

But this … no … oh!

It wasn't just that somebody had thoughtlessly folded over the page. This wasn't thoughtlessness. It was – vandalism! His lovely dandelion-yellow-haired Rosheen had been smeared and slashed with ugly tattered ribbons of paint – dense black gashes, inter- sected and smeared by screaming red and murky mustard stripes. Somebody had deliberately destroyed his picture. His paintbrush, which he had carefully propped in the jamjar, was thrown on the table, and the brownish mess of mixed paints had dried on its bristles in dirty, sticky clumps.

Oh! Rosheen all mucky now and sticky, all smears and streaks, dirty, messy, all big painty dark mess, all ruined, oh! No more dandelion-dance. No more yellow like the moon. Only dark and sticky and ruined. Look, Froggo. Lovely picture, all messed. Oh! Somebody hate Rosheen. Somebody hate Spiderboy.

Hot tears sneaked down by the side of Ricky's nose, and he wiped them impatiently away with the back of his hand.

Stupid! It's just stupid all that messing about with paints. He should be doing his lessons, or doing something useful, helping around the house or something. I'm telling you, Nancy, he is going to grow up a lazy little so-and-so if you let him spend his time dreaming and

85

painting. Painting! I ask you! If he wants to paint, he can paint the kitchen ceiling. God knows it could do with it. Ah would you stop your snivelling, you good-for-nothing little tyke and get this mess cleared up or I'll give you a real thump, one you'll really feel. That was only a little tip.

Ricky crumpled the devastated picture into a ball and squeezed all the life out of it in his fist. Then he hurled it across the kitchen, and ran out of the room and up the stairs, up and up, up and up again, right up to the attic at the top of the house. He didn't go into his bedroom. Instead he pulled open the door of the moon-chair room.

There it was, the moon chair, standing serenely among the jumble and debris of Kelly family life, all the dead old things no-one ever used any more, the tailor's dummy standing like an old and silent friend, the old manual typewriter, half of whose keys stuck if you tried to depress them, an abandoned and rather beautiful crystal chandelier spilling out of a box like solidified raindrops. The crocheted blanket was still there, hanging on the back of the moon chair. Ricky pulled it aside and gazed at the chair, its graceful, tapering back pointing up to the attic ceiling, as if straining to reach out through the roof and to the sky, and topped by the amazing moon-shaped image. He looked at the friendly, bottom- shaped wooden seat, the gleaming, curvaceous arms and he sat down carefully in the moon chair and pulled the rug over him.

Then he remembered Froggo. He reached into the

inside pocket of his jacket and pulled him out by the back leg. He draped Froggo carefully on the arm of the chair, and then he waited, stroking Froggo's velvety back, for the moon king feeling to start.

The attic room began slowly to revolve about him as he sat. The tailor's dummy leant towards him, the lampshade swaying drunkenly, its fringes brushing his cheek, as if it was about to kiss him. Just in time, it lurched backwards again and stood up straight, but then the old typewriter started to slide down the desk, as if it was going to land in his lap, and the disused chandelier shook its rainy hair out of its box and tinkled a little silvery laugh, so that sparkles flew from it and danced around the room, bouncing off the walls like shooting stars. Enchanted, Ricky watched the twinklings flying and falling, whirling and swirling, whizzing now in a mad, twirling rainbow, and he was riding the rainbow, the dusty, sticky-keyed old typewriter now on his knee, its old keys suddenly alive and fluent, clacking merrily as if the typewriter was trying to type something. Ricky's fingers found the keys, and now he was typing. TEH MOOON kiNG he typed. He was the moon king, he was, he was, he was!

Ricky really was the moon king now. Here in this room, in this chair, he was in charge. Whoever had spoilt his picture, whoever hated him, couldn't touch him here. Here it was just him and Froggo and the moon chair and all the abandoned things in the moon-chair room, and he was flying.

This was where the junk was put, cast aside, the things other people didn't want. Ricky was king of the junk, king of all the abandoned things, and he was flying. Here he ruled. Nobody could bully him here, nobody could beat him or tell him he was good for nothing, and he was flying.

The room started to slow down now and gradually came to a standstill. Ricky himself came slowly to land in the moon chair. The wild tinkling of the chandelier slowed to a ripple and finally stopped, the flying glitters settling into a still but scattered rainbow pattern cast here and there over the walls and floors and objects in the room.

As Ricky touched down, balancing the old typewriter on his knees, the lampshade-headed dummy bent towards him again, bowing towards her king. King Ricky raised his hand graciously to show her he was listening, ready to consider her request, but she was too shy to speak. Never mind, said Ricky to her. You don't have to speak if you don't want to. Some other time perhaps, and the lampshade nodded its fringes, coyly hiding the shy dummy-lady's face. Not at all, waved Ricky. Think nothing of it.

The crystal chandelier gave a final wavering clink from its box on the floor and settled its sugar-stick tresses. Everything was calming down, getting ready to rest at Ricky's royal feet.

Ricky! Ri-ii-icky! Ricky! Ricky!

The voice came to him from very far away, but it was

getting nearer. A clear, bell-like voice. He didn't answer. He wanted to hear the voice again.

Ricky! Are you up there? Come on down. Ri-ii-icky!

The voice was getting nearer. Ricky shook himself and sighed. What was that weight on his knees? He looked down at the typewriter. It was battered and bashed-looking, and a funny smell came off it, like mildew. His finger was on the letter G. Gingerly he removed the finger, but the key stayed down. Ricky heaved the typewriter back onto the desk, and as it hit the desk, the G key bounced back up. A little puff of dust rose up from the keyboard as it did so, and Ricky sneezed. He gathered Froggo off the arm of the chair, where he had managed to maintain his balance all this time, and stood up, as a shadow appeared in the doorway.

'Ricky!' said Rosheen now in an ordinary voice, no longer having to shout because she was almost beside him. 'Was it you who left that mess on the kitchen table? Did you know you'd spilt the water? It was all brown, like mud, only more liquidy, and there's a pool of it on the kitchen floor. And the paintbox is open and some of the paints have the lids left off and there isn't even a picture! What have you been doing? It's lucky it was you. If any of the rest of us did that, Mammy Kelly would have our lives. Come on down now and help me to clean it up before teatime. Didn't you paint a picture after all? How could you have made such a mess without painting anything?'

Rosheen prattled on, not pausing for Ricky to answer

her, even if he had wanted to. But that didn't matter. He didn't want to. He just wanted her to go on and on, chattering and warbling, like the pigeons. He wasn't listening to what she was saying any more, just following her down the stairs and listening to the sound her voice made, like chiming in the wind.

'And then when we get it all cleared up,' Rosheen was saying, 'we'll just have time to feed the pigeons. Would you like that? We can do it together if you like, but we'll have to hurry because we must get that mess out of the way first, or there'll be blue murder, I'm telling you, absolutely blue blooming murder!'

CHAPTER 16

Ricky Goes into Hiding

'I told you I'd tell your social worker about how you have been bullying me,' Helen hissed.

It was some time after the destroyed picture episode. Helen and Ricky and Rosheen and Fergal were in the front room, the one full of hatstands, where Ricky had slept on his first night in the Kellys' house. Fergal was having a go on the exercise bike and the others were sitting looking out the window at the rain. The children often sat here, especially on rainy days, or when they were expecting a visitor, because there were deep windowseats and once you cleared the junk off them you could get a good view of the weather or of anyone struggling up the front garden. You didn't walk up that front path, you climbed up it. It was always a struggle, because the garden was on such a steep slope.

And sure enough, as Helen spoke, the nondescript bundle of clothes that was waddling up the steps towards the house came suddenly into focus. Several raindrops converged in a particular spot on the window, swimming together to form a temporary lens of rainwater, just level with Ricky's vision. As he peered through the little lens of water, the figure clarified as that of the Lipstick Woman. Ricky sat stock still, his throat dry, his skin crawling, as the little knot of raindrops suddenly dispersed and ran in separate rivulets down the window.

'How do you know that's his social worker?' Fergal gasped, still pedalling, and peering over the others' shoulders.

'I'm telling you. I asked her to come. I thought she ought to know about how badly he's been behaving,' said Helen smugly, kicking with her runners against the panelling of the windowseat.

'Badly? Ricky behaving badly? What are you talking about?' This was Fergal again. 'And don't kick the panelling, Helen. It's all scuffed already from people doing that. You know Ma hates it.'

Rosheen said nothing. She had seen the look of horror on Ricky's face.

'"Don't kick the panelling. It's all scuffed already,"' Helen repeated in a silly sing-song copycat voice. 'You're so stupid, Fergal. If it's all scuffed already then it doesn't matter if I kick it some more, does it, dummy?'

'Yes it does, fat-head, because it gets worse,' retorted Fergal. 'Anyway, Ricky doesn't know how to behave badly. We all know who's the specialist in bad behaviour around here. Miss Greeneyed Sourpuss.'

Helen pouted, but she didn't argue. She didn't need to. It looked as if she was getting her way.

'Anyway,' Fergal puffed on, 'she wouldn't come just because you wanted her to come. She's coming on one of those regular visits they do so that they can go on being paid. She wouldn't listen to you.'

Helen just grinned. 'You wait and see, then, Mr Smartypants Fergal. You just wait and see. She's going to take him away. She knows he isn't suitable for a decent family like this, a juvenile delinquent like him.'

'Juvenile delinquent!' Fergal laughed. 'You don't know what you're talking about. Ricky's not a juvenile delinquent.'

'Then what's he doing living here?' Helen challenged him. 'If he's just an ordinary boy, why doesn't he live at home with his mother and father like normal people?'

'He hasn't got a father, Helen,' said Fergal. 'You know that. It was all explained. And his mother's in hospital. He's just here until she's better and can mind him again herself. You know there's always a reason kids come here, but it's not because they're juvenile delinquents. For goodness' sake, get a grip!'

Ricky looked at him curiously. Was his mother going to get better and mind him? Did that mean he had to go home? And would Ed be there still? If Ed was going to be there, he wasn't going home, he wasn't. Even if Ed wasn't there, even if it was just going to be him and his mother, he wasn't sure he wanted to go home. He loved his mother, but she hadn't stopped Ed. She hadn't been strong enough. She hadn't had the guts. He half-thought she believed Ed when he said what a bad boy Ricky was. She must believe him if she went on letting him hit Ricky so often. She must think he needed to be beaten. Maybe he *was* a bad boy. Ed thought so. Helen thought so.

'Shut up, Helen,' said Rosheen through clenched teeth.

'I don't see why I should shut up. I haven't done anything wrong. I just asked the nice lady to come and take this nasty little boy away. That's perfectly reasonable.'

'You're nuts,' said Rosheen. 'If you think we're going to believe you did that, you really are nuts. You're just saying it to frighten Ricky. You hate it when new people come, don't you? Even Billy, little Billy – you were jealous of him when he came. You think your mother belongs to you, don't you? I think it's time you grew up and started to act your age. So just give it a rest, would you, and leave Ricky alone.'

'"Leave Ricky alone",' repeated Helen in her put-on sing-song, high-pitched voice. 'Poor Ricky, he can't answer back, so everyone has to talk for him. I don't see why he can't speak up for himself anyway. All this no-talking business, it's pure affectation, that's what it is, pure affectation. He's well able to talk if he wants to.'

Affek-tay-shun. Ricky wondered what it meant. Affek-tay-shun.

'Three miles,' said Fergal, mysteriously. 'I've just cycled three miles.'

'Don't be silly,' said Helen, 'you haven't moved.'

'The equivalent of three miles, then,' said Fergal. 'Who else wants a go now? You could do with a bit of exercise, Helen. You only ever walk from the fridge to the telly and back.'

Ricky slid down from the windowseat and slipped out of the room while the other three were arguing about the exercise bike. He took the stairs two at a time, his heart thumping against his ribs as he climbed swiftly up and up, staircase by staircase. He was on the half-landing where the bird-mobile swung silently above the rocking- chair when he heard the ding-dong of the doorbell. He didn't stop to hear if it was answered. On he climbed, up and up to the moon-chair room.

Wish Spiderboy had crack to hide in. Scuttle, scuttle. Hide! Hide! Lipstick Woman coming, take Spiderboy away. Spiderboy don't want go home. Ed still there. Mam, oh Mam! Spiderboy want stay here. Spiderboy want stay in this house. Nice people. Mother-person nice, fun. Santy-man big and strong but nice to Spiderboy. Rosheen your good friend. Oh, moon chair. You are the ... No! No! No more moon king! Just Spiderboy. No moon chair. No moon king. Aaagh! Aaagh!

Ricky gave way to tears. He didn't understand what was happening. All he wanted was to be left alone. He didn't want to fight with Helen. And he didn't want to go home, not if Ed was still there. He wanted to see his mother, but he didn't ever want to see Ed again, and if Ed was at home, he didn't want to be there. Ed would beat him again, especially if his mam was still away in the hospital. He beat him even when she was at home, but it would be much worse if she was away. No, he couldn't go home, he just couldn't. He had to hide. He had to avoid being sent home. He had to. Somehow. But where could he hide? Where would he be safe?

CHAPTER 17

Where's Ricky?

Mammy Kelly burst into the front room, skirts swishing, bracelets jangling, Billy bouncing in her arms. Billy put his arms out when he saw Rosheen and said, 'Wo-wo!'

'Rosheen!' exclaimed Rosheen. 'Did you hear that? He said "Rosheen".'

'That's not "Rosheen",' said Helen scathingly. 'That's "water".'

'Wo-wo!' Billy declaimed again, waving his little starfish hands at Rosheen and leaning out towards her.

Mammy Kelly thrust Billy at Rosheen who gathered him delightedly into her arms.

'Where's Ricky?' Mammy Kelly asked, looking from child to child.

Fergal looked at Rosheen. Rosheen looked at Helen. Helen looked at Fergal.

'He was here a minute ago,' Rosheen said. 'I didn't notice him leaving the room. Did you, Ferg, Helly?'

'Don't call me that!' snapped Helen. 'It's a stupid name.'

'Hah!' said Rosheen, 'Helly Kelly, you're a poem!'

'Girls, girls, stop squabbling. Helen, will you go and find Ricky please. He needs to be here. I have Mrs O' Loughlin in the kitchen now and she wants to talk to him.'

'I'll go, I'll go,' Rosheen offered. 'I know where to find him.'

She didn't want to mention the moon-chair room, though she was pretty sure that's where she'd find him. She couldn't bear the thought of the grown-ups charging up to the top of the house and raiding Ricky's special room. She could just imagine Mammy Kelly poking around in the crystal chandelier box, stirring the crystals with her pudgy fingers until they shivered; tripping over the lady with the lampshade hat and not even knowing to say 'Excuse me'; smashing her way around that treasure trove that was Ricky's special place, without even understanding about the moon king or anything, without knowing what it all meant. No, the best thing was to go after him herself and get him down, before anyone else started poking around up there.

'No, I'll go,' said Helen.

'No, let me,' Rosheen pleaded.

'Ma told me to go,' said Helen, elbowing Rosheen out of the way, 'and I know where to find him too. In fact, I'd *like* to find him. I want to tell him he's wanted down in the kitchen by Mrs O'Loughlin.'

'Oh, let her go, Rosheen,' said Mammy Kelly. 'It's not a big deal, after all. It's just a routine visit.'

'Oh, I think *Ricky* thinks it's a big deal,' said Helen.

'I hope Ricky is happy with us,' said Mammy Kelly with a worried look, taking Billy back from Rosheen and hoisting him up on her hip. 'I thought he had settled in very well. He doesn't want to tell Mrs O'Loughlin that he doesn't like it here, does he?'

'I couldn't tell you what he wants to tell her,' said Helen with a toss of her head. 'But whatever it is, he'll have to do it in sign language, won't he?' And she flounced out of the room, calling, 'Ricky! Ricky! You're wanted! It's your social worker!'

Mammy Kelly shook her head and left the room with Billy, a frown puckering her forehead. She knew Helen had been dead set against Ricky when he first came, but she'd had a long chat with her about it all, and she thought Helen had got over it. But now it didn't look as if they'd made peace at all.

Helen barrelled up the stairs, still singing out 'Ricky! Ricky! It's your social worker!' That should get him good and worried, she thought meanly.

She arrived on the first half-landing where the rocking-chair was nodding away like some demented old person. She put out a hand to steady it because it was making her seasick and anyway, she needed to stop for a rest. It was true she didn't get enough exercise.

On the first full landing she stopped again to get her breath and then lumbered on, up past the bird-mobile, which was swinging and dipping slowly, to the second full landing. She stopped again. It was very quiet up here. She had been able to hear the voices of the other children playing in the front garden on the last landing, but they were completely inaudible now. The top part of the house was like a different country, still and deserted, the air warm and heavy, the carpet muffling Helen's footsteps. She toiled on up to the last landing before the attic floor and then took the final flight of stairs slowly.

On the attic level, Helen was met by perfect stillness and two shut doors. She knocked loudly on Ricky's bedroom door and marched in, still calling Ricky's name.

But he wasn't there. The room was tidy and orderly and perfectly still. She stepped over to the wardrobe and took a quick look inside. Ricky didn't have many clothes, and all that ever hung here were a pair of jeans, a few shirts and Ricky's zip jacket. The wire clothes hangers rattled as she opened the door and the jeans and shirts swung slowly and forlornly in the current of air caused by her quick movements. No jacket, though. Had Ricky been wearing his jacket? She couldn't remember.

Impatiently, Helen slammed the wardrobe door closed. She looked under the bed. No Ricky. She checked behind the door and behind the curtains. The room was so tidy, there was nothing else to hide behind or under.

Shaking her head, Helen came out of Ricky's room and peered in all the dusky corners of the landing. He must be in the junk room, she thought with a sigh. She knew he'd been using it as a sort of den. She'd followed him up here on a few occasions, hanging back out of sight on the stairs, and seen him go in there. But that room was so full of stuff, he could be hiding anywhere in it. Helen was beginning to regret having volunteered to find Ricky. Now she was going to have to climb over things and get dust up her nose. She put her hand on the door handle and pushed, but the door wouldn't give. Drat the boy! He'd locked himself in.

'Ricky, come out of there this minute,' Helen called through the keyhole. 'Come on, now, you can't keep Mrs O'Loughlin waiting. She's a busy woman.'

Silence.

Helen threw her shoulder against the junk-room door, to make a noise, but there was no answering scrabbling from the other side of the door.

'Ricky!' Helen called imperiously. 'Open up! You're only making things worse. Don't be such a scaredy cat. Come out and face the music.'

Silence.

'Ricky, I know you're in there. There's no point in hiding.'

Silence.

Helen began to get worried. Maybe he wouldn't open the door and she'd have to go down and tell them and there'd be a big scene and it would all come out that Helen had been teasing him about Mrs O'Loughlin and she'd be in trouble. That could mean no telly for a whole week. Helen tried a different tack.

'Ah, come on, now, Ricky. It's all right, really. I was

only pulling your leg about Mrs O'Loughlin taking you away.'

Silence.

'I mean, look, I know you're not a juvenile delinquent, not really. That was just a joke. Come on, now, be a big brave soldier and come out. I'll bring you down to them. Mrs O'Loughlin's very nice. You're not in trouble, Ricky. It's OK.'

Maybe he'd done something stupid. Maybe he'd jumped out of the window. Maybe he'd hanged himself! Helen broke out in a sweat.

'Ricky, I … I … I'm sorry. I … I … I … I was only teasing. I didn't mean to scare you.' Helen knew that was a fib. 'Not really,' she amended.

Silence.

Then she heard a sound. Helen breathed a sigh of relief. Something was stirring on the other side of the door.

But no, the sound wasn't coming from the other side of the door. It was coming from behind. Helen spun round. Rosheen was coming up the stairs. That was all she needed, Miss Perfect on the scene.

She turned to Rosheen with a scowl.

'He's locked himself in. He won't come out.'

'I'll get him out,' said Rosheen.

Oh yeah? thought Helen, but she knew that if anyone could, Rosheen could probably do it, so she just said: 'OK, but make it quick then, or they'll be up after us.' Right, she thought. Let Rosheen sort this one out.

Rosheen pressed her face to the door and spoke urgently into the crack between the door and the doorjamb. 'Ricky!' she called. 'It's only me, Rosheen. Open up.'

No reply.

'Look, it's OK. Mrs O'Loughlin is only here on a routine visit. She just wants to say hello and ask you how you're getting on. Don't mind Helen and her stupid stories. She's only trying to scare you. She's such a baby! Ouch!'

The last bit was in reaction to a kick on the calf from Helen. 'Go away, Helen,' she hissed over her shoulder. 'I can't make him come out if you hang around here.'

Helen gave a shrug and set off downstairs.

'Come on, Rick, open up,' Rosheen pleaded. 'Helen's gone now. I sent her downstairs. Let me in.'

Still nothing.

'Ricky? Are you in there?'

Nothing.

Rosheen rattled the door handle. 'Please, Ricky! For me. I'm worried about you. I just need to know you're OK. I won't make you come down if you don't want to.'

Silence.

Rosheen slid down to the floor and sat hunched there, her back leaning against the door. She listened very intently, trying to hear if Ricky was breathing on the other side of the door, but the harder she listened, the more she could hear her own breathing. She held her breath for a while, to see if that would help, but when she did that, all she could hear when she strained to listen was the beat of her heart.

She sat with her chin resting on her knees and tried to work it out. Maybe Ricky wasn't in there after all. But then why was the door locked? It didn't make sense.

'Ricky, Ricky, oh please Ricky, I beg of you to answer me! You don't have to come out. You don't have to open the door. Just say something, so I know you're there and you haven't run away. Anything.'

Oh, he doesn't talk, Rosheen remembered. 'Hum something, Ricky. Or tap with your feet on the floor, anything to make a sound, so I know you're there and you're OK.'

She thought again. 'I won't tell the grown-ups where you are,' she offered as the final inducement. 'I promise I won't. You are the moon king, Ricky! If you're my friend, just make a sound, please.'

Was that a sigh? Rosheen's ear was right against the door. No, it hadn't been a sigh, she was sure of it. Not a sound, not a word, not a tap, not a breath.

Suppose he's not in there, Rosheen thought. But then what was the explanation for the door being locked? She slid onto the floor, her back to the door and her forehead resting on her knees, and wrestled with the problem. It could be that he'd locked it from the *outside*, she thought, but why would he do that? What on earth would be the point? And anyway, if he had, where was he now?

CHAPTER 18

Spiderboy Sleeps

Nice, dark here, quiet. Spiderboy like dark, like quiet, like soft floor, no people, just your friends going sleep. Nice crack for Spiderboy crawl into. Cover up now for warm.

Lipstick Woman not find Spiderboy here. Spiderboy not go home. Mam go home from hospital now want Spiderboy home. Not good. Ed home. Ed not like Spiderboy. Ed want hurt Spiderboy all times. Ed hurt Mam too. Ed not hurt Mam if no Spiderboy home. Mam and Ed good friends no Spiderboy. Spiderboy make Ed cross. Mam not make Ed cross no Spiderboy. Spiderboy better stay here your friends. Your friends like talk and sleep, that all, and eat. Just talk and sleep and eat. Spiderboy can eat that too. Spiderboy no talk like your friends, but like listen soft sounds, no shouting no screaming no doors slam.

Spiderboy like sleep now. Tired now, all that stuff. Eyes sore.

Not cry any more now, safe here. No more big tall house

all stairs. No more moon chair. Not moon king no more, silly game. Just Spiderboy now here your friends. Cover up now some more, more warm. Warmy make yawny, eyes tired, so much tears all dried up now, so sleep. Sleep, Spiderboy now. Sleep.

CHAPTER 19

Humouring Mrs O'Loughlin

'Another cup of coffee, Mrs O'Loughlin?' Mammy Kelly offered. She'd been trying to entertain Mrs O' for the past quarter of an hour, and she was running out of things to say to her. Ricky hadn't turned up. He must be in the house somewhere, but none of the children had been able to root him out. It was a bit embarrassing. It made Mammy Kelly look like the kind of person who went around *losing* children.

'No thanks, Mrs Kelly. I don't really drink much coffee. It's so hard on the system, isn't it?'

'Tea then?' asked Mammy Kelly. 'We have chamomile tea, or hibiscus, or raspberry leaf. Would you like some raspberry leaf tea, Mrs O'Loughlin? Or Pearl Grey? I mean, Earl Grey. We call it Pearl Grey. Family joke, you know. We think it sounds like one of those colours they make up on colour charts, you know, the ones the paint companies do? Like Buttery Yellow, Ice Blue, Applewood.' Mammy Kelly knew she was burbling, but she was desperate to fill up the silence. 'Zanzibar,' she added lamely, 'though goodness knows, that could be anything.'

'No, no. Nothing at all, thank you.'

Mammy Kelly started. What was the woman on about? Oh yes, the tea. She was refusing a cup of tea. What on earth had made her rabbit on about paint charts? She must pull herself together. The woman would think she was a crackpot.

Mammy Kelly looked around the room. What could she offer this woman, to take her mind off the fact that the child she had come to see was missing? Well, not missing exactly. Just temporarily mislaid.

'A brownie? Would you like a chocolate brownie?'

'I'd love a chocolate brownie,' intervened Helen, coming into the room. 'Can I get the tin?'

'I suppose so,' answered Mammy Kelly. 'They're home-made, you know,' she went on enthusiastically to Mrs O'. 'I only give the children home-made cakes and biscuits. Well, at least that way you know what's in them, don't you? Ah, Rosheen, there you are, girleen. Did you find Ricky?'

Rosheen had appeared in the doorway behind Helen, looking disconsolate. She shook her head.

'He's not in his room,' she said. 'Or anywhere upstairs. I don't know where he's got to.'

'Well,' said Mrs O'Loughlin, standing up and brushing imaginary crumbs off her lap, 'I suppose there's not much point in my staying any longer if you can't find the boy.'

'Oh it's not that we've lost him or anything like that,'

said Mammy Kelly. 'He must be somewhere about. He was here ten minutes ago.'

'*I* was here ten minutes ago,' said Mrs O'Loughlin with unnecessary accuracy, Mammy Kelly thought, 'and he wasn't here then.'

'Oh, well,' she mumbled. 'Twenty minutes ago, maybe.'

'I'll be back at the same time tomorrow,' said Mrs O'Loughlin stiffly. 'Maybe you could arrange to have Ricky here to meet me then.'

'Oh yes, certainly,' said Mammy Kelly fervently, delighted the woman was going and the embarrassing situation was coming to an end.

'But in the meantime, I am a bit concerned that nobody knows where the boy is,' Mrs O'Loughlin went on, ignoring Mammy Kelly's broad smile, 'so I must ask you to ring me as soon as he turns up. I'd like to know that you have found him before I go to bed tonight. Otherwise I won't sleep easy. Have you got my mobile number?'

'Oh, I didn't know you had a mobile,' said Mammy Kelly, trying to sound impressed.

'Yes, well, in this job it's important to be available night and day. It's a full-time job, you know.'

'Yes,' agreed Mammy Kelly. 'I know it is. No rest for the wicked, is there?'

'I don't know about the wicked, Mrs Kelly,' said Mrs O'Loughlin primly. 'In this case it's the virtuous for whom there is no rest.'

'The virtuous, yes, ha-ha, the virtuous!' Mammy Kelly forced herself to laugh, inwardly kicking herself for uttering that foolish cliché. 'Yes, yes, the virtuous. Of course. Who else?'

CHAPTER 20

Break-in

Later that evening, Helen was helping Mammy Kelly to get the tea.

'Has Ricky turned up yet?' her mother asked, handing her the breadboard. She was starting to get worried.

'No,' said Helen, guardedly. She didn't want too many questions asked about why Ricky had gone and hidden himself away.

'But it's, oh, getting on for an hour since anyone saw him,' said Mammy Kelly, handing her the breadknife as well. 'Be careful with that, lovey,' she added, automatically. It was what she always said when she gave anyone the breadknife. 'Where did you look for him, that time?' she went on.

'Oh, just around,' said Helen airily, tossing her hair over her shoulder as she peered into the crumby depths of the breadbin. 'Which loaf, Ma? The brown or the white?'

'Oh, cut them both,' said her mother. 'They're like the lion and the unicorn in this house,' she added, somewhat irrelevantly. 'Around where?' she added, determined to find out more about Ricky. An hour was a long time for a child to be missing. 'Where did you look, I mean?'

'His room, you know.'

'Is that the only place you looked?'

'No-o-o,' said Helen reluctantly.

'Well, then, where else?'

'Well,' said Helen, 'I did try the other room up there, you know, the junkroom?'

'The junkroom? What possessed you to try that old dump?'

'Oh, I don't know,' lied Helen. 'I just thought maybe he was up there. But anyway, the door was locked.'

She hadn't meant to let that slip out. Her mother was bound to find that suspicious.

'The door of the old junkroom was locked?' her mother repeated, incredulously. 'But who would lock the junkroom?'

'Maybe it was just stuck,' said Helen, not too sure why she was fibbing about this. It was probably going to come out about her teasing Ricky anyway, at this stage, and hedging like this wasn't going to make much difference.

'But don't you see,' said her mother, light dawning, 'if the door is locked, that probably means Ricky's locked himself in there!'

Brilliant powers of deduction! thought Helen witheringly. But she said, as if carelessly, 'Oh, do you think so?'

'Yes, of course I think so. He's got to be there. He's

nowhere else about the house. I checked all the other rooms. Why on earth would he go locking himself in the junkroom?' Her forehead was all runnelled with thought. 'Oh the poor little scrap! He must be worried about something. It couldn't have been that he didn't want to see Mrs O', could it, Helen?'

'How would I know?' replied Helen, sawing vigorously at the brown loaf. 'It could be anything. He's not the full shilling, is he?'

'Don't talk like that, Helen,' her mother reprimanded her.

'Sorry,' Helen mumbled. She knew she wasn't supposed to use expressions like that about children who came to the house, no matter how obvious it seemed to her that they weren't right in the head.

'Look, let's go and get him, will we?' said Mammy Kelly, taking off her apron, as if she was going on an outing. 'Come on, just the two of us.'

'Ummm,' said Helen. 'You go. I'll finish cutting up the loaves.' She didn't want to be there when her mother winkled Ricky out of the junkroom.

'Ah no,' said Mammy Kelly, 'come on with me.'

Helen couldn't think of an excuse, so she put her breadknife down and followed her mother, stifling a sigh.

In the hall, they met Tomo.

'Ricky's locked himself in the attic,' Mammy Kelly told him.

'What'd he do that for?' asked Tomo.

'Well, I don't know. Maybe he didn't want to meet Mrs O' today.'

'Why not? He doesn't usually mind her.'

'Well, I don't know, but come on anyway.'

The three of them trooped up the stairs to the first half-landing. As they did so, the bathroom door opened and Lauren came out, wiping her hands on her skirt.

'No towel,' she said apologetically. 'Where's everyone going?'

'To the attic,' Mammy Kelly replied. 'Ricky's locked himself in up there.'

'Oh?' said Lauren in surprise. 'Is that where he's got to? Can I come too?'

But she was talking to their backs. They'd got as far as the landing now. Lauren joined the trail.

Billy was sitting on the landing, carefully pulling his socks off.

'How did you get here?' asked Mammy Kelly, swooping down to pick him up. Billy gurgled and offered her a sock.

Upwards they went, the four of them and the baby, to the attic floor.

But there was no reply when they knocked on the door and called out Ricky's name. They rattled and shouted and yelled, but still there came no reply.

'Goodness, I hope he hasn't had an accident or anything!' said Mammy Kelly. 'There are all sorts of yokes in there. They might be dangerous. Quick, Tomo, break the door in. Quick, quick!' There was panic in her voice. Helen stood behind her and bit her nails.

Tomo stood back from the attic door and then he lurched at it. It shuddered, but didn't give. He lurched again. This time there was a groan of splitting wood. At the third lurch the lock broke away from the door and the door swung inwards.

Inside the attic room, the tailor's dummy stood quietly, its lampshade hat perfectly still on its head; the musty old typewriter sat motionless on the rickety old desk; the crystal chandelier spilled silently, as if frozen in time, over the edge of its cardboard box; the multicoloured blanket drooped emptily over the moon chair; the moon itself balanced in endless, perfect stillness on the point of the chair back. Not a breath was breathed, not a sigh was sighed, not even the air stirred. There was no sign of Ricky.

CHAPTER 21

A Living Duvet

Rosheen clattered her bucket of feed and her water jug as she went off to feed the pigeons. She could hear the sounds of Mammy Kelly cooking the tea as she closed the back door behind her. The evening was chilly, with more than a hint of autumn in the air, and there was that cold, sweet smell of grass you get when the dew starts to fall. Rosheen shivered inside her jacket.

Rosheen usually had Ricky's help with this chore in the evenings – sometimes he did it for her – but he hadn't turned up yet, since he'd disappeared this afternoon, so she thought she'd better get on with it. It would soon be too dark to see out there, and besides, it was past their feeding time.

Rosheen had decided not to worry about Ricky just yet. He'd reappear at teatime, she told herself. It wasn't time to start panicking. Nobody else was too concerned, though it had been embarrassing when they couldn't find him for Mrs O'Loughlin. But the locked attic door puzzled Rosheen. She could have a good think about it while she was with the pigeons. She often did her best thinking out there in the company of the birds.

They'd be hungry, Rosheen thought, as she was so late feeding them. She'd better open the door carefully or they might mob her.

But the pigeons didn't come rushing towards her as she'd expected when she entered the shed. Maybe they're getting sleepy, thought Rosheen. It's almost dark.

It took a moment for her eyes to adjust to the gloom in the pigeon shed, and when she could finally make out shapes, she saw that the perches were bare, the bird-boxes empty. All the birds were huddled in one corner, in a great heap, like a giant, living duvet. They warbled and burbled a bit as she approached, and shifted their wings, as if to get more comfortable, but otherwise they didn't move. They certainly didn't come flying towards her. Softly she moved nearer to where the birds were huddled. What was it they were huddling over?

The birds set up a mild conversational cooing as she came closer, as if to say, Ah there yoooou arrre, Roosheen. But still they didn't come to feed.

Rosheen came right up to them and knelt on one knee to examine the pile of birds and then she started to wave her hands gently, to encourage them to move. Languidly, a few of the birds on the outside layer of the huddle flew up to their perches. Rosheen spoke out loud then, and waved her arms some more. 'Shoo,' she said gently. 'Go on, shoo off there and let me see. Shoo, shoo, shoo.' Another layer of birds rose lazily from the pile and circled the shed, and then another and another, until the air was filled with the soft beatings of pigeons' wings and finally Rosheen could see a shape that wasn't birds. It was like a pile of clothes thrown on the sawdust floor.

'Ricky?' she whispered. 'Ricky, is that you?'

The pile of clothes, still wearing the occasional pigeon, moved, like a slice of swissroll gradually unwinding. Relief flooded Rosheen. She hadn't realised how worried she was until the worry lifted, but now she could feel her blood surging around her body, singing with relief. Her toes tingled with it, her scalp prickled with it. Her head ached with relief, her heart pounded with it, her ears rang with it.

'Oh Ricky!' she said, a little more loudly this time.

Ricky sat up, covered in feathers white and grey and brown and with gobs of bird-goo dotted here and there. Rosheen reached out and brushed away the remaining birds with the backs of her hands. They flapped away from her, but one bird, the small one called Fudge, came fluttering back immediately and took up residence on Ricky's shoulder. Rosheen tried whooshing him away again, but he came back as soon as she stopped, so Rosheen gave up and started to pick clumps of feathers out of Ricky's clothes. His hair was all stuck about with feathers too.

'You look like an Indian chief,' said Rosheen. 'The last of the Mohicans! How long have you been out here? Have you been asleep?' He must have been. She could tell from the muzzy look he gave her.

Ricky just stared at her, his eyes huge and black, his face pale as a pigeon's underbelly.

'Ricky, you weren't planning to stay out here all night, were you?'

Ricky looked away.

'Ricky, you'd freeze to death out here. Even the birds knew that. They must have been trying to keep you warm. But it's only teatime. Can you imagine what it would be like out here by midnight! And why did you lock the attic door? You did lock it, didn't you?'

Ricky nodded.

'But why, noodle-head? Why?'

Ricky shrugged. Fudge sat on his shoulder and rode up when he shrugged, like a seagull on a wave.

'To make us think you were in there?' Rosheen asked. 'So we wouldn't go looking for you?'

Ricky wrinkled up his forehead. Clearly, this hadn't occurred to him.

'No?' asked Rosheen. 'That wasn't it? Well then?'

Ricky sighed.

'To keep someone out, maybe?'

Ricky gave the tiniest nod, almost as if he was afraid to admit it.

'You knew Helen knew that room was your special place?'

He nodded again, this time a series of short, quick, affirmative nods.

'And you didn't want her in there?'

A slow nod, this time, followed by another one.

'You are the oddest person, Ricky,' said Rosheen, tenderly. 'I mean, you do the oddest things. But look, it's teatime. You must be starving. Help me to feed the birds now, and then we'll go in for something to eat.'

Ricky hunched himself right up, drawing his knees quickly up under his chin and shook his head vehemently from side to side.

'And you can see Mrs O'Loughlin tomorrow instead. She said she'd be back.'

Ricky shook his head vigorously. A little shower of sawdust fell out of his hair and sprinkled his shoulders. Fudge stepped back delicately and shook his head a few times, to rid himself of the sawdust-raindrops. Ricky put a hand up and gently fingered Fudge's feathers, to calm him.

'Ricky, you have to see her,' said Rosheen. 'She's in charge of you. But that doesn't mean she's going to take you away. That was just Helen saying that. She was only trying to annoy you.'

Ricky cowered back from her, though, shaking his head.

She wasn't getting through to him. That was clear.

'But, look,' Rosheen said, 'you can't stay here. You'd die of the cold.'

Ricky turned away from her and faced the wall. He put his hands over his ears.

Rosheen thought for a moment. There was no point in arguing with him. Maybe the best thing was to leave him be for a little while. She stood up and busied herself about the shed, feeding the birds. They gathered around her as she filled their grain troughs and poured their water.

Still Ricky sat with his back to Rosheen, staring at the wall, his hands clamped over his ears and his elbows sticking out on both sides of his head. When she'd finished the feeding, Rosheen came and sat beside him.

'Ricky!' she bellowed at him, at the same time trying to prise his hands off his ears. Ricky resisted, and there was a bit of a scuffle. In the end Ricky dropped his hands stiffly to his sides, but he still faced the wall. He wouldn't look at Rosheen.

Rosheen tried a different tactic.

'You must be hungry, Ricky,' she said.

Ricky continued to stare at the wall. Rosheen looked at his thin little back, still covered in feathers and goo. She couldn't let him stay here. It just wasn't on. He'd freeze or starve or both. She'd have to persuade him to come into the house. But not yet. He was too frightened. Oh dear, oh dear, oh dear!

Spiderboy hungry, yes.

'I'll tell you what, I'll bring some food out. We'll have a little picnic out here, just the two of us, and we can talk a bit more then. You'll feel better if you have something to eat. OK?'

Not a sound out of Ricky. Not a movement.

Spiderboy hungry. But Spiderboy want stay here your friends, no house, no bully girl, no Lipstick Woman.

Rosheen put her hand on his shoulder and said: 'I'll be back. Just give me fifteen minutes. Don't move, Ricky, OK?'

Ricky sat absolutely still.

CHAPTER 22

Food for Ricky

The kitchen was deserted when Rosheen came in from the pigeon shed, but the tea was half-ready. The bread had been cut anyway, she saw.

Swiftly, Rosheen buttered and halved a slice of brown and a slice of white and sandwiched thick orange slices of cheese between the halves. Then she looked around for something else. She scooped up two apples and a banana from the fruitbowl on the kitchen counter and wrapped two chocolate brownies in a square of tinfoil. She couldn't find a small bottle to put a drink in, so instead she filled a mug with milk and carried it carefully to the back door. Then she had to put everything down to open the door, as her hands were full.

She'd only been about ten minutes in the house, but when she got back to the pigeon shed, there was no trace of Ricky, apart from a bare patch in the sawdust where he'd been sitting facing the wall when she'd left.

'Oh no!' said Rosheen aloud to the pigeons. 'Now where's he got to?'

Then she sat down on the floor and put her hands

over her face. She felt a cry trying to get up her throat and out her mouth, but it got stuck somewhere and left her with a filled-up, chokey feeling that was worse than tears.

CHAPTER 23

Tea-time

Tea was a silent meal in the Kelly household that evening. By now, everyone knew that Ricky had disappeared. Not everyone realised how serious that was, but everyone got the message that the grown-ups were worried.

Everyone except little Billy, who sat in his high-chair and banged his spoon loudly. People were supposed to take notice when he did that. Sometimes they cheered him on; sometimes they told him to hush up and give them a bit of peace. Tonight they just ignored him. He couldn't understand why. He tried banging a bit harder, but still he got no reaction. Then he banged very loudly and very rapidly, but the only reaction was that Mammy Kelly leant over and prised the spoon out of his fingers.

Billy started to cry. Not very loudly. Not to get attention. Just because everyone was acting so strangely and it frightened him.

'He never misses his tea,' said Mammy Kelly, to the table at large, to no one in particular, to anyone who would listen.

'He'll be back when he gets hungry,' said Lauren,

trying to comfort her. 'Boys always do.' She pulled Billy out of the high chair and put him on her knee and fed him small pieces of bread and butter off her plate. He chewed them slowly, tears still glistening in his eyes.

Rosheen said nothing, but she glared over her teacup at Helen. Helen said nothing either.

'Maybe you're right,' said Mammy Kelly, but without much conviction. 'Maybe so.'

Thomas and Seamus and Fergal looked sagely at their plates and thought they wouldn't miss their tea for anything. But then, they weren't Ricky. Ricky was different.

The small ones ate quickly and quietly, using both hands efficiently and taking advantage of Mammy Kelly's absentmindedness to stuff too much food into their mouths at once, but for some reason they didn't really enjoy it, not even the brack with thick white icing on top with cherries in it. They didn't even squabble about the jam or anything, just passed each other things silently, sensing that something was going on.

Tomo wasn't at tea. He'd taken the van and gone to search around the town for Ricky. After they'd found the attic empty, Mammy Kelly and Tomo had decided that Ricky was really missing. They were going to have to ring Mrs O'Loughlin, they'd decided. Then Rosheen came in from the pigeon shed and told them he'd been there ten minutes earlier, but he was gone now.

To Rosheen's surprise, that cheered them up. 'He

can't have got far in ten minutes,' reasoned Tomo.

'Well, maybe fifteen minutes,' said Rosheen, trying to be accurate. 'Or even twenty.' But they weren't really listening to her.

'No need to ring Mrs O' just yet, in that case,' Tomo said.

Instead, he rang his friend Terry and the two of them sped off down the town in the van.

'We'll give it half an hour,' Tomo said over his shoulder as he left the house. 'If you don't hear from us within half an hour, you can ring her, Mary.'

Mammy Kelly nodded, holding on to the front door as if for support, and waving Tomo goodbye as he went down the garden steps, as if he were going on his holidays.

CHAPTER 24

The Search

Tomo and Terry kept their eyes peeled as they drove into town, stopping occasionally and shining the headlights deliberately onto the verge and into the ditch, but they didn't see Ricky on the road. When they got to town, they did the round of the cafés and fish-and-chip shops, the snooker hall, the youth club, the amusement arcade (though Ricky was far too young to be let in there), the scout den, the petrol stations and the open-till-late minimarkets. It was a Thursday night, so some of the bigger shops were also open late. They wondered if Ricky might have dipped into a shop to avoid being seen. They had a look in the main ones, and they asked the security men and shop assistants, but they were big places where a boy might easily hide. Nothing.

Then they tried all the churches, because some of them were open in the evenings, and they thought a youngster might feel safe in a place like that, but there was no sign of Ricky.

When they'd exhausted all the indoor possibilities, they started looking on the streets, peering into parked cars and vans and lorries, down alleyways, in doorways, behind the hoardings on vacant sites. They even looked in a skip, pushing aside a roll of damp carpet and a couple of lengths of metal piping. Terry knew of a few derelict houses, some of which were used as squats, and they did the rounds of those too. They met a few people in the squats, some of whom were friendly, though they looked pretty battered, but nobody admitted to seeing a kid as young as Ricky. They tried under the railway bridge, where a gang of teenagers was gathering early for a cider party and in the public toilets in the square, where an old man washing his feet in the washbasin gave them a sour look. They walked along the riverbank and poked in the long grass and the bedraggled hedgerows, but there was no sign of Ricky.

They went back towards the busier end of town then and looked in another skip and on the backs of lorries. They even did a round of the pubs, though neither of them could imagine Ricky being let into any of them. The pubs were quite full, because people had come in for a drink on their way home from work and there was music in some of them. They tried the loos and cloakrooms too.

Then Terry remembered that the local dramatic society was holding a dress rehearsal of their annual play in the town hall, which meant that that building would be open, so they drove around to there and interrupted the rehearsal to ask the actors if they'd seen a small, thin, scared boy, but nobody had. They tried the store-rooms and dressing rooms backstage, and the producer even let them into a cavernous space under the stage, which was full of orchestral instruments and trunks of theatrical costumes, but to no avail. Disconsolately, the two men drove back along the dark streets, peering at every figure they spotted on the pavement. The early show at the cinema had started by then, but Tomo parked the van opposite so they could have a good view of anyone sneaking in late. No Ricky.

They pulled in at a phone box, to ring home and report no progress. 'I think it's time to go ahead and raise the alarm,' Tomo said to his wife. 'Ring Mrs O'. And the guards, I suppose.'

With a heavy heart, Tomo returned to the van.

'What about the hospital?' Terry asked.

'You mean he might have had an accident?' said Tomo. 'I never thought of that.'

'Well, yes, that's a possibility, but did somebody say his mother was in hospital? Maybe he went looking for her.'

'You could be on to something,' said Tomo, changing gear and heading for the hospital, on the outskirts of town.

But there was no sign of Ricky there, either prowling the wards or in the small casualty unit, and the only small boy who'd been treated all day was somebody called Gary who'd been in with a dislocated shoulder. The staff all knew him, because he was always dislocating his shoulder.

'What about his home?' Terry asked as they got back into the van.

'The social worker will have somebody out there looking for him as soon as she hears,' said Tomo. 'There's no point in our going there too and complicating matters. It's miles away, anyway. I can't imagine him getting there, unless he got a lift. I hope to God he hasn't been hitching, though.'

Terry nodded grimly. They both knew the dangers there were for kids on their own.

After some more fruitless searching, Terry went home. It was getting late, and he hadn't eaten yet. But Tomo kept on doggedly looking, looking.

The evening wore on and started to turn to night, and there was no sign of Ricky anywhere in the town. As the early show at the cinema ended, Tomo examined the streams of people coming out of it. No sign of a small lad creeping out among the grown-ups. He stood on a corner for a while, watching the queue forming for the later show, but there were no children to be seen. They were all at home doing their homework or getting ready for bed by now.

Tomo paced the main streets again and again, his hands thrust into his pockets and his collar turned up against the cold. He met a garda patrol car and hailed it, to tell them, but they knew already.

'We're going to do a circle of the town and try the barns and byres in the outlying farms, Mr Kelly,' said Guard Lynch. 'There's a few of our lads on foot already on the lookout. If we don't find him by morning, we'll have to mount a formal search.'

If we don't find him by morning! Tomo shuddered at the thought, but he just nodded to the guard and said 'Right, Guard, good night now,' and the patrol car purred off down the street, its blue light flashing occasionally.

CHAPTER 25

Rosheen's Nightmare

Rosheen was truly worried by now. She sat in a tiny darkened room at the back of the house, supposedly watching television. Mammy Kelly deliberately put the TV in the pokiest and most uncomfortable room, because she thought TV viewing should be confined to programmes you wanted to see so desperately you were prepared to put up with any discomfort to watch them.

The children had all crowded into the TV room this evening, but Rosheen couldn't follow the programme: it was just a succession of meaningless images and booming sounds to her. She sat in the gloom, her eyes prickling with unshed tears, imagining the things that might have happened to Ricky. He'd been gone a good three hours, and his disappearance was officially a crisis by now. Mrs O'Loughlin was discussing the situation with Mammy Kelly, and Guard Lynch had called in to take a description.

Ricky might have gone home, Rosheen thought. The guard had asked something about that when he was here. She didn't know where Ricky's home was. All she knew was that his mother was in hospital. Maybe she was home now, and maybe she was glad to see him. That would be nice, a happy ending. But somehow, that didn't really seem to fit. It was like doing a jigsaw and having a piece that is almost the perfect shape for an awkward gap, but no matter how you turn it around and try to ease it in, it just doesn't quite slip into place. She didn't know much about how these things worked, but she knew Ricky couldn't just run home and it would all be OK.

She hardly dared to think of the other things that might be happening to him. He might have run off into town and be hanging around the streets, cold and hungry, looking for a doorway to sleep in, terrified in case the police might find him, or that drug-pushers or bad people might get hold of him. He might have been kidnapped by a gang of criminals and be all tied up with tape over his mouth in the boot of a car. He might have dashed out on the road in a panic and been run over by a hit-and-run driver and be lying bleeding to death in a ditch. He might have been abducted by aliens and taken to another galaxy and be being debriefed right at this very moment by the alien chieftain – not that they would get much out of Ricky. Anything might have happened to him!

And the worst part of it was, no matter where he was, he probably really believed what Helen had said, that he was going to be sent away, that the Kellys didn't want him. But that wasn't true. Rosheen was sure Mammy Kelly and Tomo wanted him. She'd seen them watching him with careful, worried looks. She'd seen how they made space for him when the other children crowded round and how they spoke quietly together sometimes when he left the room. She'd watched Mammy Kelly's smile growing when she bent over his shoulder to look at one of his pictures, her hand firmly on his shoulder, and she'd heard Tomo carrying on those cheerful, one-sided conversations, to which Ricky's only contribution was the occasional nod or shy smile.

Fergal liked him too, and Lauren. She knew by the way they picked him for teams when they were playing games. Thomas and Seamus didn't take too much notice of him, but they threw things at him and kicked his ankles when they passed him on the stairs or in the hall, and with them, that counted as affection, and when they played football up and down the garden before tea they shouted at him and passed the ball to him. The younger ones took him totally for granted and asked him to tie up their shoelaces for them or to mind their teddies when they were busy with other things. Billy had taken a special shine to him, crawling around after him sometimes and grabbing the cuffs of his jeans with his plump, sticky fingers, though Ricky didn't seem to notice. Helen was the only one who went out of her way to make things difficult for him.

And Rosheen herself, well she... she supposed she loved him, really, though she hadn't thought of it like that before. She felt her face getting hot thinking those words, but it was true, she did. If loving somebody is worrying about them when they were unhappy and being glad to see them when you come home from school and them making you smile just thinking about them, well then, yes, she loved Ricky. Oh dear! This time a tear really did trickle down the side of Rosheen's nose and she dabbed at it quietly with the cuff of her shirt.

Her head felt suddenly full and aching and her whole body felt weary, as if she'd been doing very hard work all day, digging the garden or cycling uphill. Her limbs ached and her bones felt heavy. She closed her eyes against the flickering dark of the TV room and rested her head back against the armchair. Maybe if she could just doze off for a few minutes, she would feel better. It felt better already to have her eyes closed and not to have to follow the movements on the screen. The noise of the TV sounded more distant, like underwater burblings.

Lulled by the sounds of the television, Rosheen fell asleep, her mouth dropping open and her chin falling onto her chest. She woke with a start a few times, dreaming that she was falling off trains or into a hole. She closed her mouth when she woke up but it soon dropped open again and eventually she drifted into a deeper sleep.

This time, she had a more elaborate dream. She was searching, searching, searching for Ricky, climbing all the stairs to his room and calling his name. She opened his wardrobe and out jumped a giant frog, as big as a calf, and shouted 'Tribberr! Tribberr!' right in her ear. She started to run down the stairs and the giant frog came bounding behind her. She ran and ran, but her legs weren't moving, she was always on the same step of the stairs, no matter how hard she ran, no matter how high she kicked her heels, and all the time the frog was shouting 'Tribb-err! Tribb-err!' in its deep base voice, so that it seemed to sound in her chest.

Suddenly she was in the garden, running still, running, running, and Ricky was there ahead of her. She could just see his back, his spiky little shoulder blades showing through his thin jacket. 'Ricky!' she called. 'Wait, it's me,' but Ricky ran on and on and she couldn't catch up with him, though she kept glimpsing him, always ahead. Then she was in the attic room, sitting on the moon chair. 'I shouldn't be here,' she thought. 'This is Ricky's chair. I shouldn't be sitting here. I can't be the moon king. I must get him. I must find him. If I don't, Mrs O'Loughlin will put him in a children's home and Helen will get him and ... Oh!!'

The tailor's dummy with the lampshade hat suddenly leant over, took off her hat and leered at Rosheen with the round, shiny face of Helen. Rosheen screamed and screamed. She screamed so loudly she woke herself up and then she screamed some more, because when she opened her eyes, she was looking straight into the round, shiny face of Helen.

'Rosheen! Rosheen! Wake up!' Helen was hissing at her. 'Stop screaming. You're dreaming. It's just getting to the exciting part.'

Rosheen looked wildly around. She was sitting in a chair, but it was a lumpy old armchair that had been relegated to the TV room and the face looming at her out of the semi-darkness was Helen's. She shook herself.

'What? What exciting part?' she asked.

'In the movie,' said Helen. 'And close your mouth. You're dribbling.'

'Oh!' said Rosheen and wiped her chin with her cuff. It was true. She had dribbled.

Rosheen lay back against the chair, still paralysed with fright, for a few moments, still half-caught in the nightmare. At last she managed to unglue her fingers from each other and bring her hand up to her face. Her hair was damp with sweat, and her clothes were sticking to her body. She combed her shaking fingers through her hair and smoothed it behind her ears. Then she tried to concentrate on the film. But it didn't do any good. No good at all.

CHAPTER 26

The Stranger

As soon as Rosheen had gone to get the food, Ricky left the pigeon shed. He knew she'd be back in a few minutes and he had to get away immediately, or she'd only stop him. He had to get away, before they came after him. Ricky didn't have a clear idea any more what it was that he was afraid of, but his instinct was to run and run and run.

It was almost dark as he slipped out the front gate. He didn't know where he was going, but he didn't care, as long as it was away from the town. So he headed off away from the lights, towards the countryside. Maybe he could find an old barn or something to sleep in.

He knew he was heading in the right direction, into the country, because after a mile or so the houses started to thin out and there were no streetlights any more and no footpath. He could smell the cold, fresh smell of fields and he could hear the sounds of animals rustling and munching and breathing in the darkness.

Ricky was scared. He was scared of the dark, he was scared of the animals he could hear around him in the fields, he was scared of the occasional cars that sped past, casting a blaze of light in front of them and forcing him to crouch in the ditch, partly to avoid being knocked down and partly to avoid being seen. Most of all he was scared of being caught and of being sent home.

Also, he was cold and he was starting to get hungry. He'd missed his tea. He had an apple in his pocket, he remembered, left over from goodness knows when. He took it out of his pocket and looked at it. He should really save it, as he was bound to get even hungrier later in the evening, but by then, he reasoned, a watery old thing like an apple wouldn't be much good to him. He might as well eat it now. Without stopping to argue with himself any more about it, he bit into the apple. The skin was wrinkled – the apple had been in his pocket for some days – and the bite of it was cold against his teeth, but the juice ran sweet and delicious and he enjoyed it.

Tossing the core into the ditch, Ricky trudged on. Now that he'd eaten his only piece of food, he felt even hungrier than he had felt beforehand. Also, there was nothing more to occupy his thoughts except his sorry situation. He wondered about his mother, whether she was still in hospital or whether she'd been sent home by now. He hadn't known she was in hospital, until somebody mentioned it. She wasn't in hospital when he'd left home. Mrs O'Loughlin had explained that his mother 'needed a break' and that was why he was going away. She'd said his mam might be able to have him back when 'things were better at home'. He hadn't really understood what that meant, but he was glad to be going away for a while, where he wouldn't have to live with Ed, although he knew he'd miss his mam.

Ed wasn't always mean to him, he had to admit that, sometimes he was nice, sometimes he bought him sweets and once he'd brought a video home for him, though it was one Ricky'd seen before; but he got very mad sometimes and then he started roaring at him and sometimes he hit him and it hurt, and then Ricky's mam would cry and cry. Ricky didn't know which was worse, being hit or hearing his mam cry. He wished she wouldn't cry, but he wished she would stop Ed hitting him too. He and his mam used to be such great friends, before Ed came. Now she was always upset about something, and worried about him annoying Ed, though he tried not to, and things weren't the same.

He wished they could have the old days back again, but his mam said that a boy needed a father and she needed a man, and he should try to make the best of it. He did try, but he didn't think he needed a father that badly.

Thinking about home made him fidgety, and being fidgety made him walk faster, and walking faster made him warm up a bit and also the effort of it kept his mind off feeling hungry, so he kept it up, walking faster and faster, and concentrating on walking fast gave him something to do.

He must have been concentrating very hard on keeping up the pace, because he didn't notice that he was no longer in the countryside until he was almost in the town. He wondered what town it could be. Could he have walked all the way to the next town already? Or had he made a half-circle around the outskirts and arrived back near where he'd started out? Yes, he thought he had, because he recognised this street, he was almost sure. It led into the centre.

Part of him was cross with himself for having arrived in town, because of the lights and everything, but another part of him was glad about it, because it was nice not to be alone in the countryside with just the cows munching in the fields and the cars streaking past. He allowed himself to slow down and look around a bit.

His attention was caught by a bakery shop with a brightly lit window, full of goodies. He stopped and stared in at the things to eat, his mouth watering and his tummy rumbling.

Cake shop here, look Froggo, oh, all cakes and doughnuts. Chocolate cake. Happy Birthday to You! Muffins. Jammy cakes. Creamy. Buns. Oh! Face in window! Shoo, Spiderboy! Just looking, just looking. Run, Spiderboy, run.

Ricky ran the length of the street and dodged around the corner to the next street.

Run, Spiderboy, run, run, run. Heart thumpety-thump, thumpety-thump, thumpety- thump. Must – stop, can't –

breathe, side sore. Oh-oh-oh. Stop heart, stop, slow down, let breathe. Oh, oh, oh. Side sore. Stand still, just breathe, just breathe.

Spiderboy tired. Like sit down now. No chairs here in street. All people, people everywhere, and cars. Everything hurry, hurry. Everybody go home now, not Spiderboy, Spiderboy no home now. Spiderboy want Mam.

Standing at a corner, holding his side, Ricky suddenly spotted a familiar figure coming towards him.

Look, Froggo, look! Santy-man! Big man, beard. Santy-man! Run, Spiderboy, run.

Ricky turned and ran and ran. His heart beat so hard it hurt. His breath came in painful gulps. Tears of perspiration ran down his face from his hair. His face was hot and red and wet. His body felt weak with the effort of running, but the big, bearded man was still behind him. He didn't dare to look back to make sure, but he could hear the steady thump, thump, thump of his feet, heavy on the pavement. Ricky was lighter and quicker, but the big man had more stamina. Ricky darted in and out between shoppers and commuters, tripping over baby buggies and shopping trolleys but managing to keep on his feet. Surely he would shake off his pursuer if he just kept weaving in and out, in and out between the people.

He came to a street corner and stopped to think about which way to go. Across the road and on, or around the corner? As soon as he stopped, his ankles turned to jelly. He put his hand out and steadied himself against a traffic-light pole. Now his legs were shaking uncontrollably. He leaned his back against the pole, for more support, but it didn't work. Slowly, his legs gave way under him and he slithered down the length of the pole and sank into a shivering heap on the footpath.

Nobody stopped to see if he was all right. Hurrying shoppers didn't notice him, and he was oblivious to them, his eyes closed, gasping for breath and glad not to be on his sore, tired feet any more. Then he heard it, the thump, thump, thump of the large, bearded man approaching the corner where he lay slumped against the foot of the pole. He forced himself to open his eyes. There was the huge man, high above him, stopped at the corner and looking around. Ricky shrank into himself, waiting for the heavy hand to fall on his shoulder, for Tomo to pull him to his feet and … he didn't know what came next. Presumably Tomo would take him back to the tall, tall house and then the social worker would be called and he'd have to go home, or worse.

But the heavy man didn't bend down to him. He didn't seem to notice Ricky. He looked up and down the street and around the corner, and cursed to himself. As he turned his head and Ricky caught sight of his face in the glow of the traffic light, he saw that it wasn't Tomo! It was a big man, but he didn't even have a beard. Ricky must have imagined it, or perhaps it had been a trick of the light.

He whimpered with relief. The man who wasn't Tomo heard the whimper and looked down at Ricky, shivering at his feet. He hunkered down to him, his huge bulk like a small mountain between Ricky and his view of the world.

'Gary!' he said, taking Ricky by the shoulder and peering into his face.

Ricky shook his head.

'You're not Gary!' the big man said in surprise.

Ricky shook his head again.

'So why were you running away from me then? Gary is always trying to give me the slip. Thinks it's a game. I should have known it wasn't Gary. He hasn't got a jacket like that. I suppose I just instinctively chase after any youngster I see running through the streets!' The big man elbowed Ricky in the ribs and gave a laugh. 'Well, look, come on anyway and I'll buy you a Coke. You look as if you could do with a drink.'

Ricky shook his head again. He didn't want to go anywhere with this stranger. He knew you weren't supposed to go anywhere with strangers.

'Or a sandwich? How about a nice ham sandwich and a cup of tea?' the man offered.

Ricky was very hungry. A ham sandwich sounded nice.

'Or maybe a burger and chips?' said the man.

Stranger. Strangers bad. Spiderboy no like strange man not Santy-man. Mam say all times, no take sweets from strangers. Burger-'n-chips not sweets, but. Spiderboy hungry. Spiderboy like burger-'n-chips.

Slowly, Ricky nodded his head.

'That's my lad,' said the big man, encouragingly, and held his hand out to help Ricky up. Ricky took the hand and levered himself up onto his feet.

'How come yer ma lets you out on your own at this hour of the night?' asked the big stranger.

Ricky shook his head.

'Hmmm,' said the man. 'Yer ma doesn't know where you are, does she?'

Ricky shook his head again.

'Hmmm,' said the man again. 'Run away, did you?'

Ricky looked up at him with huge eyes, trying to make up his mind if this man was nice or nasty, friendly or dangerous.

'Well, well, well,' said the man thoughtfully. 'Come on, so, and we'll get some grub into you.'

He didn't mention the guards or social workers or anything like that, but it was the thought of a nice hot meal that really decided Ricky. Happily, he put his thin little hand in the man's big meaty one and trotted off with him into the cold evening.

CHAPTER 27

Helen and Rosheen

The film was over. The younger children had gone to get
ready for bed. Fergal and Lauren were in the kitchen, fin-
ishing their homework. Only Rosheen and Helen were
left in the TV room. They'd switched off the telly and put
on the light, and they sat disconsolately in two uncomfortable armchairs, on either side of a cold and empty fire-
place.

'Well, I hope you're happy now,' Rosheen said
bitterly, at last.

'I'm not,' Helen retorted. 'I'm not happy at all.'

'Oh?' Rosheen was surprised. 'You've managed to get
rid of Ricky. Not content with teasing him and bullying
him to pieces, you've finally managed to frighten him
away altogether. You have the house full of guards and
social workers. You have Tomo off down town all evening
searching for Ricky. You have poor Mammy Kelly
half-demented with worry. A fine piece of work I'd call
that, Helly Kelly. You have a right to be proud of yourself.'

'I'm not, I'm not. I'm not proud and I'm not happy.
How often do I have to say it? Why won't you believe me?'

'Why won't I believe you? I wouldn't believe the Lord's Prayer out of your mouth, Helen, so I wouldn't, because you're not capable of telling the truth. You wouldn't know the truth from a ... from a ... from a superannuated wombat!'

'A *what* sort of a wombat?'

'Oh, it doesn't matter!'

'Oh Rosheen, I'm sorry,' said Helen.

'You're what? You're sorry? Well, a fat lot of use that is now, Helen. Sorry won't bring Ricky back. Sorry won't solve the mess you've got this whole family into.'

'No, but still, I *am* sorry,' snivelled Helen. 'I am, I am.'

'Oh, I'm sure you're sorry all right,' retorted Rosheen. 'You're sorry you've let it get this far, because you're bound to get into trouble. It's all going to come out now, about the misery you made Ricky's life, and I'm quite sure you're sorry about that, because you are going to be in mega-trouble, so you are. Well, that's one thing about this whole miserable situation I'm not sorry about, because you have it coming to you.'

'I didn't mean to be mean to Ricky,' Helen said.

'Yes, you did,' said Rosheen.

'Oh, OK, OK, you're right, I did mean it,' said Helen. 'But, but, but ... I didn't *want* to mean it, or at least ... I don't want now to have meant it.'

Rosheen said nothing.

'If you see what I mean,' Helen added desperately.

'No, I don't see what you mean,' said Rosheen coldly.

'You're making it hard for me, Rosheen,' said Helen.

'Why shouldn't I?' retorted Rosheen.

'Because I'm *sorry*,' said Helen. 'That's why.'

'But sorry isn't enough. I told you that.'

'Well, it's all I can do for now,' said Helen. 'And I'm not just saying sorry. I *mean* sorry.'

'Oh well,' Rosheen shrugged, as if she'd had enough of this tedious conversation.

'There you go again,' said Helen.

'What?'

'There you go again. I'm trying to talk to you, and you're off someplace else, not listening to me. It's been like this ever since Ricky came. You never listen to me. You never talk to me. All you want is Ricky, Ricky, Ricky. You don't want to play house or school or anything any more, nothing but Ricky and those flippin' pigeons.'

'Oh!' Rosheen was startled. Was she like that? 'Well, I like Ricky,' she said.

'Everyone likes Ricky. What's so great about Ricky?'

'Well,' began Rosheen thoughtfully, 'he's sad and he's upset, but he doesn't make a fuss about it. He just gets on with things. He tries. He smiles. He does his painting and he helps out around the place and he just does his best, even though things are hard for him. He's not always worrying whether people like him or not. He just tries to get along as best he can, without causing too much trouble.'

'Oh? Is that it?' Helen was genuinely surprised to hear

what it was that made people like Ricky.

'Yes, and he doesn't hurt people or upset them or look for notice. He keeps his problems to himself. He's just ... sweet!' She stuffed the back of her fist up against her mouth as she said that, so she wouldn't cry.

'Sweet!' Helen echoed. How do you learn to be sweet? she wondered. 'He's sweet,' she said again, softly, to herself, as if trying this idea on for size. 'It's all my fault, isn't it?' she said sadly then.

'Yes, it is,' said Rosheen bluntly. 'If you hadn't frightened him about that social worker, he'd never have run away. He believed you when you said she'd come for him, you know. It was such a stupid thing to say!' Rosheen could feel anger against Helen starting to build up in her again. It was like a weight gathering at the nape of her neck.

'I was only teasing,' said Helen tearfully.

'But Helen, you don't tease a person like Ricky. He doesn't understand and he isn't able to take it.'

'I know, I know. I'm sorry.'

'You can be such a bully, Helen.'

'I – just, I just didn't like him being your friend. *I* used to be your friend, until he came.'

Rosheen stared at her. This explanation was far too simple to explain Helen's behaviour. It wasn't true anyway. She and Helen had been at loggerheads for ages. But maybe it was part of the reason for it. Poor old Helen, she thought then. Nobody much liked her, and even if that was largely her own fault, that didn't make it any easier. She'd always thought it must be easier if you were really part of the family, like Helen was. It wasn't much fun only half-belonging, and knowing you had problem parents out there somewhere that you were going to have to deal with some day. But it hadn't occurred to her that maybe it was hard on Helen too, having to share her mam and dad with so many other children, having to be just one of lots instead of one of a few, having to fight for her place in the family all the time, or thinking she had to fight for it anyway.

'Well, you can be my friend again,' she said. 'There's no reason not to be. But you have to be friends with Ricky too.'

Helen pouted. She knew this would have to be the bargain, but she didn't like it.

'And don't put on that puss,' Rosheen said. 'It's no good wanting to be friends and then going all sour as soon as you are asked to do the friendly thing.'

'The friendly thing?' asked Helen. 'What's the friendly thing?' Though she knew, really she knew.

'Well,' said Rosheen, who knew too, but wasn't sure how to put it into words, 'it's about, well, it's about thinking about the other person's point of view sometimes, instead of always about yourself. It's about noticing when somebody is hurt, instead of just looking for notice yourself all the time. And it's not a competition. It's not about winning and losing and scoring points all the time; it's about letting the other person win sometimes … oh, I can't explain it without sounding like a total wimp!'

'But if you let the other person win,' said Helen, 'then you lose.'

'No,' said Rosheen. 'It's not like that.'

Helen looked at her dubiously.

'No, really. If I'm friends with Ricky,' Rosheen explained, 'I can still be friends with you, and if I'm friends with you, I don't have to stop being friends with Ricky.'

'Yes you do,' argued Helen. 'If you're friends with me, and I've been mean to Ricky, then you are saying it's OK to be mean to Ricky. You're taking my side.'

'No!' said Rosheen. 'You're just not *getting* it, Helen.'

'Is that what's wrong with me?' Helen asked. 'I don't get it?'

'No, it's not that there's something wrong with you. You can *decide* to get it, Helen.'

'Can I?' asked Helen. 'Are you sure?'

'Yes,' nodded Rosheen. 'You really can. You can decide that you want to be friends with me and with Ricky, and then all you have to do is start acting friendly.'

'Are you sure it's that simple?'

'Yes, I'm sure. Forget about taking sides and being for and against and keeping scores. Just make the decision, Helen. Just do it.'

'Oh!' said Helen. 'Oh!' It had never occurred to her before that she could just make a decision like that. She didn't know your decisions could change things, if you acted on them. It was a whole new way of thinking about things.

'OK, then,' she said at last. 'OK, I've decided.'

Rosheen looked at her and said nothing for a long time.

'Is that right?' asked Helen anxiously. 'Did I say it right?'

'Yes,' said Rosheen. 'Yes.'

'And you?' Helen went on. 'Did you decide the same?'

'Yes,' said Rosheen, with a tiny sigh. 'Yes, OK, I decided the same.'

'Oh good,' said Helen with a beam. 'Oh GOOD!'

'Only …,' Rosheen went on, 'only … only, we can't *decide* Ricky back, can we?'

'No,' said Helen, 'but maybe we could find him. Oh Rosheen, come on, let's try!'

'Where would we look?'

'Down the town,' said Helen.

'But Tomo is gone down the town, and he hasn't found him. He phoned to say so.'

'Yes, yes, but still, *we* might find him. Come on, Ro, come on, let's go!'

CHAPTER 28

Ricky Gets Away

Ricky had managed to give the man the slip. While he was eating his burger and chips the man had gone off to pay the bill. It was as easy as that. Ricky just slipped down off the high plastic stool in the burger place and sauntered off out the door, still clutching a half-eaten burger wrapped in a paper tissue, not looking left or right or back over his shoulder. Nobody stopped him.

It was cold outside the burger place, colder than Ricky remembered it being when they went in, and it was starting to rain. Ricky pulled his thin, slithery jacket miserably around himself and tried to concentrate on the rest of his burger, but it didn't seem to make him feel much better. He started walking quickly away from the burger place. He turned the first corner he came to and the next and the next, and then he started to slow down, thinking the big man would never find him now.

The rain was coming down harder. It was cold rain, like melting chips of ice beating on his head and face and making his nose run with cold and wet. Raindrops were starting to work their way down the back of his neck now.

He tried to pull his collar more closely around his neck, but still the wet seemed to find its way in.

He had to get in out of the cold and the rain, but where could he go? He didn't know anyone. He didn't even know for sure where he was. He couldn't go back to the burger joint, or he might meet the tall man. It would have to be a shop. The shops were still open and they looked all warm and welcoming, with their yellow lights glowing in the dark street.

Hunching his shoulders, Ricky sidled into a shop. The warm air hit him as soon as he crossed the threshold. It smelt good in here, clean and sweet and fresh, like a very warm, carpeted fairy bathroom, with lots of mirrors and goldy things all piled up like Christmas presents. A soft tune was playing, and every now and then the tune was interrupted by a doorbell sound, and a voice came with a mysterious message that Ricky couldn't make out. When he blinked, the raindrops on his eyelashes made tiny kaleidoscopes, and he could see the warm, yellowy shop glowing and turning in front of his eyes, like so many bright dandelion flowers.

Oh Rosheen! Wish Rosheen. So cold. Wish warm, wish your friends, wish didn't run …

The sudden warmth and sweetness made Ricky feel heavy. His eyelids were too heavy for his eyes. He wanted to sit down, but there were no seats, and anyway, he didn't want to sit somewhere where he might be noticed. He took an escalator up to the next floor and looked around. Still no seats, but there were lots of racks of coats up here.

Maybe, maybe, yes, yes, he could just crawl under one of the racks, yes, that one over by the wall, and then he could curl up and he would be hidden by the long coats, and nobody would be able to see him. He could be warm and dry and hidden in there, and he could have a rest, just a little rest, on this nice thick carpet. His feet were warm now, his hands were warm, even his nose was warm. He was like a little furry mouse all wrapped up in warmth.

All warmy dark in here, things hanging. People's feet, quiet on carpet. Voices, long way, people talking, all quiet and soft. Spiderboy just hide in here now, just rest, just keep nice warm, just lie still, no go home, no cold now, nice warm, just lie, just breathe, just still.

CHAPTER 29

Searching

Rosheen and Helen had slipped out of the tall house and half-walked, half-run into the town centre. Now they were walking the streets, looking in doorways and down alley-ways and calling Ricky's name. It was late shopping evening, so even though it was dark and long past the usual rush hour, the streets and shops were still full of people. They walked and walked and called until they were hoarse.

They stopped on a street corner. They didn't know it, but it was precisely the corner where Ricky had met the large man.

Rosheen checked her watch. 'It's almost half-past eight. The shops will be shutting soon.'

'I'm cold,' said Helen, pulling her jacket more closely around her. 'And I hate this sort of rain. It's even colder than it is wet!'

'Yes, it is,' agreed Rosheen, blowing on her fingers. 'We're wasting our time on the streets. It's too cold and wet here. He must have slipped into a building to get out of this wind.'

'But what sort of building?' asked Helen, shivering and looking hopelessly at the town around them, full of buildings, any one of which could be harbouring Ricky.

'Well,' said Rosheen, 'the offices are mostly closed, and anyway, he wouldn't get past security. I don't think he has any money, so he can't have gone to the cinema or a coffee-shop or anywhere you have to pay. And I don't think he has any friends in town, so he can't have gone to anybody's house.'

'Maybe he's in a shop, then,' said Helen.

'Yes, he must be,' Rosheen agreed. 'But which shop? There's millions – Maguire's and Casey's and O'Donovan's and Reed's and ... We're just going to have to make a start right here and keep going till we find him.'

'We probably haven't a hope,' said Helen dismally, 'but I suppose all we can do is try and trawl through as many shops as we can manage.'

'OK,' said Rosheen. 'I think we'd better split up. That way we can cover more shops before they close. Let's meet here, at Reilly's corner, at ten past nine, with or without Ricky. You take High Street and Abbey Street. I'll do John's Parade and the shopping centre.'

'Right,' said Helen. 'See you soon!' And she and Rosheen turned their backs on each other and walked off in opposite directions.

Then Helen remembered something. She stopped and looked over her shoulder and called to Rosheen's retreating figure: 'Good luck!'

Rosheen looked back and waved.

'If you see Tomo, *hide*,' she called. 'We'll be murdered if we're caught out at this time of night.'

'OK,' Helen nodded. 'Will do.'

CHAPTER 30

Home Again, Home Again

There were cars parked everywhere, at all sorts of rakish angles, outside the Kellys' house, even up on the footpath, when Rosheen and Helen got home from town that night. The house must be full of people, they thought. As they got to the gate, the front door opened and somebody came rushing down the garden path and hurtled out the gate past them without even seeing them. She jumped into one of the badly parked cars and revved off down the road without a backward glance.

'Was that Mrs What's-it from the corner shop?' Rosheen asked.

'Heffernan,' said Helen, 'Mrs Heffernan.'

The front door opened again, and another figure came out and down the path, not at quite the same speed.

'Mr Ryan,' said Rosheen, 'you know, with the small black dog, from two doors up.'

The girls stood back from the garden path in the dark of the lawn, and Mr Ryan passed them by, calling back to a figure at the door: 'Don't worry, Mary, we'll find him. Every car in the parish will be out till we do.'

Mr Ryan got into his car, put on his lights, signalled carefully, and pulled away from the kerb in the opposite direction from Mrs Heffernan.

The girls needn't have worried about getting into trouble for leaving the house so late. There was such a to-do about Ricky, nobody had had time even to notice they were missing. They waited for the front door to close after Mr Ryan, and then crept in, using Rosheen's house key, but even so, Mammy Kelly met them in the hall.

She saw two cold and bedraggled girls, their hair in rats' tails on their shoulders, their faces red and wet and streaked with dirt, their stockings spattered, their expressions dejected.

'Where were ye?' she asked, her voice puzzled rather than cross. 'Come in the pair of ye, in here to the warm, ye're frozen.' And she gathered a girl under either arm and ushered them into the front room.

The living room, normally full of things, was now full also of people, sitting and standing and milling about and all talking at a great rate, conferring and making suggestions and drawing maps for each other and waving their arms about giving each other directions. The search-party for Ricky was swinging into action. Mrs O'Loughlin was there, speaking rapidly into her mobile phone, her finger in her other ear, and Guard Lynch from the local garda station was leafing through a notebook and shaking his head.

In between the adults were all the children, making

themselves very small and keeping very quiet, because they knew something serious was going on. The smallest children, all except Billy, were huddled under a round table, which had a long tablecloth that reached down to the ground so that it was like being in a tent. They were in their pyjamas and their hair was streaked with damp from having their faces washed. The older ones sat in odd corners on the floor, leaving what chair space there was for the grownups. Somebody sat on a logbox that Rosheen had forgotten was there, because it was usually so covered with things, and one person who had managed to find herself a chair sat on top of such a pile of magazines that her feet didn't reach the floor. She had Billy on her lap, and was playing Round and Round the Garden with him to distract him from the tense atmosphere of the room and keep him from under Mammy Kelly's feet. Billy chuckled out loud every time it got to 'And tickly under there!' 'More!' he cried every time, 'more!'

Mammy Kelly picked a towel off a clothes horse that stood near the fire and threw it to Helen. 'Now,' she said. 'Where were ye? Down the town? Did you see Tomo? No sign of Ricky?'

Helen was towelling her hair, so Rosheen answered. 'No, no sign,' she said. 'I saw Tomo, he's still searching the streets. We looked in Casey's and Reed's and O'Donovan's, and I think Helen was in Maguire's too, but then it was getting late, so we thought we'd better come home. Sorry, Mammy Kelly.'

Mammy Kelly took the towel from Helen and passed it to Rosheen.

'Tea, Lauren?' she called out. 'Any tea for the girls?'

Lauren appeared from nowhere with two mugs of tea.

'Thanks,' Rosheen whispered, afraid to speak up in case she burst into tears.

'Yeh, thanks,' echoed Helen, her cold fingers closing over the warm mug.

CHAPTER 31

Jiggety-jog

The soft background music in the department store was interrupted by a chime like a doorbell; the lights flickered on and off, on and off, and a voice that sounded as if its owner had a peg on her nose announced: 'Store closing in *five* minutes. *Five* minutes, ladies and gentlemen. Please com*plete* your purchases and pro*ceed* to the *exit*-doors. And thank you for shopping with us this *eve*ning. Four and a half *minutes* now, ladies and *gentlemen*.'

Ricky uncurled himself and blinked. The message registered. They were closing up. What was he going to do now? Should he stay still as a mouse and wait for them to shut up the shop? But then he'd be locked in all night. What if he got hungry? He *would* get hungry – he was hungry already. What if he got scared? He *would* get scared in the dark with strange shapes all around him. What if there was a guard dog that they let loose in the department store at night?

No, he'd better get out of here now, while the going was good.

He stood up and brushed himself down.

But where was he going to go now? He thought about going home, but he knew in his heart he couldn't go there. Anyway, if he did go home, they'd only find him there. He thought about hanging around on the cold streets, but he'd had enough of that. It was cold, cold, cold and wet and windy, and it was scary, with strange people offering you hamburgers. They might be mean or cruel or dangerous. So what was he going to do? Maybe he should never have left the tall house. That was the only place where most people were nice to him, where they let him do his stuff and they didn't shout or make a fuss or tell him he was bad. He was still worried about the Lipstick Woman coming to take him away, but maybe Mammy Kelly wouldn't let her. Maybe Tomo would tell her to leave him be. Tomo was dead on.

Maybe better go home Rosheen's house. Even if Lipstick Woman … Well, anyway … Where else? No crack Spiderboy scuttle into now. No place at all now for Spiderboy. Best go home now Rosheen's house. Warm there, your friends, no Ed, no trouble – 'cept bully girl, she trouble all right. Oh well, come on, Froggo. Best go home. Home again, home again, jiggety-jog.

Ricky sailed off down the escalator, as the lights flickered on and off again and the peg-nose voice said something indecipherable, and came out onto the cold, wet street. He wasn't sure how to get back to the Kellys' house, but he had a rough idea how he'd got here, so he thought he'd just retrace his footsteps and keep going. With a bit of luck, he'd recognise landmarks along the way, and they would guide him home. Well, not home exactly, but the nearest place he could think of to home.

With a defeated feeling, Ricky drew the back of his hand across his face, which was still warm from the department store. Then he pulled his thin jacket closer to his body and set off.

His sense of direction must have been better than he realised, because after a long walk, he made it to the tall iron gate. He stood outside it and looked between the bars at the tall house, perched above him, over the sloping garden, a light showing in the front room, and people moving inside. It was like a picture. He was outside, looking in at people in a warm, dry, well-lit place, a place where they belonged.

Home again, home again, jiggety-jog, Froggo.

With a shrug, he pushed against the gate and opened it. Then he trudged up the garden steps, slipped around the back of the house, in the back door, into the darkened kitchen, with its night-time carrotty smell, and up the stairs, up, up, up, up to the place where he belonged.

CHAPTER 32

'I am the Moon King'

It was getting very late. The visitors had all gone home.

Suddenly Tomo, who'd given up searching in town and come home for a short rest, noticed the time. 'Bed!' he bellowed, sticking his big hairy head under the tablecloth, where the smallest children were huddled. At the sound of that word, they all came tumbling out, giggling because they'd managed to stay up so late, but secretly pleased that they could go to bed now, because they were getting sleepy.

'Tomo?' said Lauren, standing up. 'Ricky's social worker wasn't really coming to take him away, was she?'

Tomo gathered up Billy, who was already nodding, into his arms. He looked over the tiny boy's head at Mammy Kelly, and raised his eyebrows. She looked back at him, her mouth dropping open.

'What ever gave you that idea?' Tomo asked Lauren.

'Oh, I didn't really think that,' Lauren said, looking at Helen. 'I just thought maybe some people had got a confused idea.'

'Confused! Is that what you call it?' Mammy Kelly

said, looking straight at Helen also.

'Yes,' said Rosheen quickly. 'Just a misunderstanding, that's all, just a misunderstanding.'

'Hmm,' said Tomo, 'well, look, we'll talk about this in the morning. But I don't want anybody being confused. There is no question of Mrs O'Loughlin taking Ricky away, as long as he's happy here.'

'OK,' said Lauren, still looking at Helen. 'I was only asking.'

Tomo bent his knees and picked up the next smallest child also and tucked her under his other arm, while Lauren herded the rest into a bobbing little group, and off they trooped up the stairs, the ones on foot dancing along in front of Tomo and Lauren like little flowerheads.

'You too,' said Mammy Kelly to Helen and Rosheen, 'it's way past everyone's bed time,' so they stood up, said good night and followed the smaller ones up the stairs. Trip, trip, trip, went the small ones, stomp, stomp, stomp went Tomo, trudge, trudge, trudge went Helen and Rosheen, weary and disappointed after their failed search of the town.

When they got to their room, Helen turned to Rosheen: 'Let's just go up to the junkroom one last time before we go to bed.'

'It's not a junkroom,' said Rosheen. 'It's the moon-chair room.'

'Yes, well, whatever,' said Helen agreeably. 'Let's go up there anyway.'

'What for?' said Rosheen. 'I'm tired.' She didn't add that there was an awful sadness weighing on her heart, and she just wasn't in the mood for pranking around in the attic tonight.

'Well, Tomo broke the lock earlier,' Helen said. 'Let's see what the damage is.' For some reason, she badly wanted to see the moon-chair room before she slept.

'What *for*?' Rosheen asked again. 'I want to go to bed.' Not that she really expected to get much sleep.

'Ah, come on, Rosheen, let's just go up. It might … it might inspire us!'

'About what?'

'About where Ricky is, of course,' said Helen.

'I don't see how it could,' said Rosheen. 'But if you really want to, OK then. Lead on, Macduff.'

The two girls climbed to the very highest floor in the house, way up under the roof. It was dark, dark up there, and the broken door creaked over and back on its hinges.

'Put the light on,' Helen hissed to Rosheen.

'The bulb's gone,' said Rosheen.

Through the open door of the moon-chair room, Rosheen could see out the attic window. There was a streak of pale light in the night sky, reflected from the streetlights on the road. It wasn't much, but it was enough to reveal shapes in the room.

Together, the two girls moved to the door and stood looking in at the mysterious grey, huddled shapes. They could make out the tall, pointy shape of the moon chair in the grey light. Rosheen squeezed up her eyes. She could have sworn there was something stuck on top of the moon on top of the chair, something small and clumpy.

Then the crocheted blanket bundled on the chair stirred.

'It's him,' whispered Rosheen excitedly. 'Oh, you were right, Helen.'

Helen smiled in the darkness. She hadn't really been right. She hadn't expected they would actually *find* Ricky. But she had been sort of right. It *had* been her idea to come up here.

'He came *home*,' Rosheen said then. 'He came home to *us*. Oh, Helen!'

Helen grabbed Rosheen's elbow. She didn't want her collapsing up here in the dark. At her sister's touch, Rosheen turned, in the pale light, and squeezed Helen's arm. They held onto one another delightedly for a moment, searching in the half-light for each other's faces, each other's expressions.

'Remember, now,' Rosheen whispered, her mouth close to Helen's ear. 'Remember what we said earlier this evening. Don't blow it, Helen, OK, just don't blow it.'

Helen nodded. 'Ricky?' she called gently, turning to the shape on the chair, raising her voice a little so he could hear her from the landing. 'Are you awake, Rick? It's only us, me and Rosheen.'

Bully girl? That's bully girl. Spiderboy hide, no bully girl, no, no! Spiderboy no can hide here. Found.

The blanket unfurled and the silhouette of Ricky's spiky hairstyle emerged from it.

Rosheen said nothing at all. This was Helen's chance.

'Ricky?' said Helen again. 'I'm sorry I teased you. I didn't mean it.'

Rosheen nudged her in the ribs.

'I mean, no, sorry, I did mean it. But I'm sorry now, OK?'

Ricky blinked and yawned.

Bully girl sorry? For why? For sure?

Then Rosheen spoke.

'Hey, Ricky,' she said softly. 'You gave us all a terrible fright. But we're glad you came back, Ricky. We're really glad you're home, me and Helen, both of us.'

Rosheen! Oh Rosheen! Glad? Glad! Rosheen glad. Spiderboy glad. Bully girl glad too?

An arm shot up from the moon chair, the fingers all akimbo against the flat grey surface of the window, like a black handprint etched on a piece of paper. Ricky was stretching.

'Ricky, it was all lies about Mrs O' coming to get you,' Helen went on. 'I just made it up. She wouldn't take you away from here. Mam and Tomo are the best foster-parents in the county. Everyone knows that. They never take people away from here, unless they're ready to go home. Honest to God, Ricky, cross my heart and hope to die.'

Lies? Bully girl? Bully girl no tell lies now?

Then there came an unexpected sound, a whickering of wings, and the shape on top of the moon on Ricky's moonchair flapped into the air. A pale streak whirred across the room, did a quick circuit, and arrived back on its perch, over Ricky's head.

Ricky's upstretched hand did a twirl in the air, reaching up towards the bird, and Rosheen thought she could hear the sound of a soft laugh. Fudge rose into the air again, flew excitedly around the moon a few times and then settled back on the top of it and started to investigate the depths of his feathery armpit.

'You are the moon king, Ricky,' Rosheen said softly then, still standing in the doorway. 'Welcome home, moon king.'

Spiderboy welcome home? No, no Spiderboy, no Spiderboy no more. You are the moon king, Ricky.

There was a rustling and a creaking from the moon chair.

'You are the moon king, Ricky,' Rosheen repeated, a little more loudly.

The shape that was Ricky sat straight up in the chair. And then, out of the dark silhouette came the answering words in Ricky's small, piping voice: 'I – am – the moon king.'

Rosheen nudged Helen delightedly. 'Did you hear that?' she whispered. 'He's *talking*. And he's talking *right*.'

Then Ricky spoke a little more loudly, as if he was practising with his voice: 'I am the *moon* king.'

And at last, with great conviction, he flung both his arms in the air and cried: 'I *am* the moon king.'

OTHER BOOKS BY SIOBHÁN PARKINSON

CONTEMPORARY FICTION

Four Kids, Three Cats, Two Cows, One Witch (maybe)

FOUR KIDS
BEVERLEY: the bossy one, stuck up and fussy.
ELIZABETH: easy-going, a bit of a dreamer.
KEVIN: a good looker and cool dude.
GERARD: who takes his cat everywhere, and is barely tolerated by the girls.

THREE CATS Well, there's Gerard's Fat Cat, or Fat, for short. And then there are the two Pappagenos.
TWO COWS What are *they* doing in this story?
ONE WITCH (maybe) Well, is she or isn't she? Kevin seems to know but he's not telling. And what *is* a witch anyway?

The four, plus cat, set out for Lady Island, hoping for adventure, maybe even a little danger. But nothing prepares them for their encounter with the eccentric Dymhpna and the strange events that follow.

'One of the best children's books
we've ever had, full stop!'
ROBERT DUNBAR, THE GAY BYRNE SHOW

Winner of a Bisto Book of the Year Merit Award, 1998

CONTEMPORARY FICTION

Sisters ... No Way!

Two diaries in one book

When Cindy's father becomes involved with Ashling and Alva's mother, all hell breaks loose. No way will these three ever call each other sisters.

CINDY If her father thinks he can just swan off and actually marry one of her *teachers*, Cindy will show him! But worse than that are her two daughters – so prissy and boring! It's gross!

ASHLING If only her mother could find a nice man – but the new man in Ashling's mother's life comes with a daughter, the noxious Cindy, arch-snob and ultra opinionated.

'Extremely clever ... Much insight and good humour ... teenage fiction at its most sophisticated.
CHILDREN'S BOOKS IN IRELAND

WINNER of the overall
Bisto Book of the Year Award 1997

HISTORICAL FICTION

Amelia

All that matters to Amelia is dresses and parties. But when the family fortunes decline she must face hardship and poverty she has never known. And when Mama ends up in prison, what is Amelia to do?

'A tremendous read' Robert Dunbar

Shortlisted for the Bisto Book of the Year Award

HISTORICAL FICTION

No Peace for Amelia

A sequel to *Amelia*

The Great War is going on in Europe, and in Dublin the Easter Rising occurs. Amelia, now fifteen, falls in love with Frederick – but what should she do when he enlists? And servant girl Mary Ann's brother has to hide to escape being arrested for his part in the Rising. How should the girls react to these wartime activities?

'**A sparkling story**'
THE IRISH TIMES

FOR YOUNGER READERS

The Leprechaun Who Wished He Wasn't

An unusual story about a leprechaun who was fed up with being small and wants to be BIG – and a girl who feels she is too big and wants to be small!

FOR YOUNGER READERS

All Shining in the Spring

**A special book to help parents and children
through the death of a small baby**

Matthew's mother is expecting another child and Matthew is planning all the things they will do together. Then the dreadful news comes that the baby will not live. Now the family must face this huge loss.